THE GRAY
MAHATMA

THE GRAY MAHATMA

TALBOT MUNDY

WILDSIDE PRESS

THE GRAY MAHATMA

CHAPTER I

THE GRAY MAHATMA

Meldrum Strange has "a way" with him. You need all your tact to get him past the quarreling point; but once that point is left behind there isn't a finer business boss in the universe. He likes to put his ringer on a desk-bell and feel somebody jump in Tibet or Wei-hei-wei or Honolulu. That's Meldrum Strange.

When he sent me from San Francisco, where I was enjoying a vacation, to New York, where he was enjoying business, I took the first train.

"You've been a long time on the way," he remarked, as I walked into his office twenty minutes after the Chicago flyer reached Grand Central Station. "Look at this!" he growled, shoving into my hand a clipping from a Western newspaper.

"What about it?" I asked when I had finished reading.

"While you were wasting time on the West Coast this office has been busy," he snorted, looking more like General Grant than ever as he pulled out a cigar and started chewing it. "We've taken this matter up with the British Government, and we've been retained to look into it."

"You want me to go to Washington, I suppose."

"You've got to go to India at once."

"That clipping is two months old," I answered. "Why didn't you wire me when I was in Egypt to go on from there?"

"Look at this!" he answered, and shoved a letter across the desk.

It bore the address of a club in Simla.

Meldrum Strange, Esq.,
Messrs. Grim, Ramsden and Ross,
New York.

Dear Sir,

Having recently resigned my commission in the British Indian army I am free to offer my services to your firm, provided you have a sufficiently responsible position here in India to offer me. My qualifications and record are known to the British Embassy in Washington, D. C., to whom I am permitted to refer you, and it is at the suggestion of —— —— (he gave the name of a British Cabinet

Minister who is known the wide world over) that I am making this proposal; he was good enough to promise his endorsement to any application I might care to make. If this should interest you, please send me a cablegram, on receipt of which I will hold my services at your disposal until your letter has time to reach Simla, when, if your terms are satisfactory, I will cable my acceptance without further delay.

Yours faithfully,
Athelstan King, V. C., D. S. O., etc.

"Do you know who he is?" demanded Strange. "That's the fellow who went to Khinjan Caves — the best secret service officer the British ever had. I cabled him, of course. Here's his contract. You take it to him. Here's the whole dope about this propaganda. Take the quickest route to India, sign up this man King, and go after them at that end for all the two of you are worth. That's all."

My passport being unexpired, I could make the *Mauretania* and did. Moreover I was merciless to the expense account. An aeroplane took me from Liverpool to London, another from London to Paris.

I don't care how often you arrive in Bombay, the thrill increases. You steam in at dawn by Gharipuri just as the gun announces sunrise, and the dreamy bay glimmers like a prophet's vision — temples, domes, minarets, palm-trees, roofs, towers, and masts.

Almost before the anchor had splashed into the spawn-skeined water off the Apollo Bunder a native boat drew alongside and a very well-dressed native climbed up the companion-ladder in quest of me. I had sent King a wireless, but his messenger was away in advance of even the bankers' agents, who flock on board to tout for customs business.

He handed me a letter which simply said that the bearer, Gulab Lal Singh, would look after me and my belongings. So I paid attention to the man. He was a strapping fellow, handsome as the deuce, with a Roman nose, and the eye of a gentleman unafraid.

He said that Major King was in Bombay, but detained by urgent business. However, he invited me to Major King's quarters for breakfast, so instead of waiting for the regular launch I got into the native sailboat with him. And he seemed to have some sort of talisman for charming officials, for on the quay an officer motioned us through without even examining my passport.

We drew up finally in front of a neat little bungalow in a long street of similar buildings intended for British officials. Gulab Lal Singh took me straight into the dining room and carried in breakfast with his own hands, standing behind my chair in silence while I ate.

Without much effort I could see his face in the mirror to my right, and when I thought he wasn't noticing I studied him carefully.

"Is there anything further that the *sahib* would care for?" he asked when the meal was finished.

"Yes," I said, pulling out an envelope. "Here's your contract, Major King. If you're agreeable we may as well get that signed and mailed to New York."

I expected to see him look surprised, but he simply sat down at the table, read the contract over, and signed it.

Then we went out on to a veranda that was shut off from the street by brown *kaskas tatties*.

"How long does it take you to grow a beard?" was his first, rather surprising question.

It was not long before I learned how differently he could treat different individuals. He had simply chosen his extraordinary way of receiving me as the best means of getting a real line on me without much loss of time. He did not compliment me on having seen through his disguise, or apologize for his own failure to keep up the deception. He sat opposite and studied me as he might the morning newspaper, and I returned the compliment.

"You see," he said suddenly, as if a previous conversation had been interrupted, "since the war, governments have lost their grip, so I resigned from the army. You look to me like a kind of God-send. Is Meldrum Strange as wealthy as they say?"

I nodded.

"Is he playing for power?"

"He's out to do the world good, but he enjoys the feel of it. He is absolutely on the level."

"I have a letter from Strange, in which he says you've hunted and prospected all over the world. Does that include India?"

I nodded.

"Know any of the languages?"

"Enough Hindustani to deceive a foreigner."

"Punjabi?"

I nodded.

Mind you, I was supposed to be this fellow's boss.

"I think we'll be able to work together," he said after another long look at me.

"Are you familiar with the facts?" he asked me.

"I've the *dossier* with me. Studied it on the ship of course."

"You understand then: The Princess Yasmini and the Gray Mahatma are the two keys. The Government daren't arrest either, because it would inflame mob-passion. There's too much of that already. I'm not in position to play this game alone — can't afford to. I've joined the firm to get backing for what I want to do; I'd like that point clear. As long as we're in harness together I'll take you into confidence. But I expect absolutely free rein."

"All right," I said. And for two hours he unfolded to me a sort of panorama of Indian intrigue, including dozens of statements of sheer fact that not one person in a million would believe if set down in cold print.

"So you see," he said at last, "there's something needed in the way of unobtrusive inspection if the rest of the world is to have any kind of breathing spell. If you've no objection we'll leave Bombay tonight and get to work."

Athelstan King and I arrived, after certain hot days and choking nights, at a city in the Punjab that has had nine names in the course of history. It lies by a winding wide river, whose floods have changed the land-marks every year since men took to fighting for the common heritage.

The tremendous wall, along whose base the river sucks and sweeps for more than a third of the city's whole circumference, has to be kept repaired by endless labor, but there are compensations. The fierce current guards and gives privacy to a score of palaces and temples, as well as a burning ghat.

The city has been very little altered by the vandal hand of progress. There is a red steel railway bridge, but the same framework carries a bullock-road.

From the bridge's northern end as far as the bazaar the main street goes winding roughly parallel with the waterfront. Trees arch over it like a cathedral roof, and through the huge branches the sun turns everything beneath to gold, so that even the impious sacred monkeys achieve vicarious beauty, and the scavenger mongrel dogs scratch, sleep, and are miserable in an aureole.

There are modern signs, as for instance, a post office, some telegraph wires on which birds of a thousand colors perch with an air of perpetual surprise, and — tucked away in the city's busiest maze not four hundred yards from the western wall — the office of the Sikh apothecary Mulji Singh.

Mulji Singh takes life seriously, which is a laborious thing to do, and being an apostle of simple sanitation is looked at askance by the populace, but he persists.

King's specialty is making use of unconsidered trifles and misunderstood babus.

King was attired as a native, when we sought out Mulji Singh together and found him in a back street with a hundred-yard-long waiting list of low-caste and altogether casteless cripples.

And of course Mulji Singh had all the gossip of the city at his fingers' ends. When he closed his office at last, and we came inside to sit with him, he loosed his tongue and would have told us everything he knew if King had not steered the flow of information between channels.

"Aye, *sahib*, and this Mahatma, they say, is a very holy fellow, who works miracles. Sometimes he sits under a tree by the burning ghat, but at night he goes to the temple of the Tirthankers, where none dare follow him, although they sit in crowds outside to watch him enter and leave. The common rumor is that at night he leaves his body lifeless in a crypt in that Tirthanker temple and flies to heaven, where he fortifies himself with fresh magic. But I know where he goes by night. There comes to me with boils a one-legged sweeper who cleans a black panther's cage. The panther took his other leg. He sleeps in a cage beside the panther's, and it is a part of his duty to turn the panther loose on intruders. It is necessary that they warn this one-legged fellow whenever a stranger is expected by night, who should not be torn to pieces. Night after night he is warned. Night after night there comes this Mahatma to spend the hours in heaven! There are places less like heaven than *her* palace."

"Is he your only informant?" King demanded.

"Aye, *sahib*, the only one on that count. But there is another, whose foot was caught between stone and stone when they lowered a trapdoor once in that Tirthanker temple. He bade the

Tirthankers heal his foot, but instead they threw him out for having too much knowledge of matters that they said do not concern him. And he says that the trapdoor opens into a passage that leads under the wall into a chamber from which access is obtained by another trapdoor to a building inside *her* palace grounds within a stone-throw of that panther's cage. And he, too, says that the Mahatma goes nightly to *her* palace."

"Are there any stories of *her*?" King inquired.

"Thousands, *sahib*! But no two agree. It is known that she fell foul of the *raj* in some way, and they made her come to this place. I was here when she came. She has a household of a hundred women — *maunds* of furniture — *maunds* of it, *sahib*! She gave orders to her men-servants to be meek and inoffensive, so when they moved in there were not more than ten fights between them and the city-folk who thought they had as much right to the streets. There was a yellow-fanged northern devil who marshaled the serving-men, and it is he who keeps her palace gate. He keeps it well. None trespass."

"What other visitors does she entertain besides the Mahatma?"

"Many, *sahib*, though few enter by the front gate. There are tales of men being drawn up by ropes from boats in the river."

"Is there word of why they come?"

"*Sahib*, the little naked children weave stories of her doings. Each has a different tale. They call her empress of the hidden arts. They say that she knows all the secrets of the priests, and that there is nothing that she cannot do, because the gods love her and the *Rakshasas* (male evil spirits) and *Apsaras* (female evil spirits) do her bidding."

"What about this Tirthanker temple? Who controls it?"

"None knows that, *sahib*. It is so richly endowed that its priests despise men's gifts. None is encouraged to worship in that place. When those old Tirthankers stir abroad they have no dealings with folk in this city that any man knows of."

"Are you sure they are Tirthankers?" asked King.

"I am sure of nothing, *sahib*. For aught I know they are *devils*!"

King gave him a small sum of money, and we walked away toward the burning ghat, where there was nothing but a mean smell and a few old men with rakes gathering up ashes. But outside the ghat, where a golden mohur tree cast a wide shadow across the road there was a large crowd sitting and standing in rings around an absolutely naked, ash-smeared religious fanatic.

The fanatic appeared to have the crowd bewildered, for he cursed and blessed on no comprehensible schedule, and gave extraordinary answers to the simplest questions, not acknowledging a question at all unless it suited him.

King and I had not been there a minute before some one asked him about the Princess Yasmini.

"Aha! Who stares at the fire burns his eyes! A burned eye is of less use than a raw one!"

Some laughed, but not many. Most of them seemed to think there was deep wisdom in his answer to be dug for meditatively, as no doubt there was. Then a man on the edge of the crowd a long way off from me, who wore the air of a humorist, asked him about me.

"Does the shadow of this foreigner offend your honor's holiness?"

None glanced in my direction; that might have given the game away. It is considered an exquisite joke to discuss a white man to his face without his knowing it. The Gray Mahatma did not glance in my direction either.

"As a bird in the river — as a fish in the air — as a man in trouble is the foreigner in Hind!" he answered.

Then he suddenly began, declaiming, making his voice ring as if his throat were brass, yet without moving his body or shifting his head by a hair's breadth.

"The universe was chaos. *He* said, let order prevail, and order came out of the chaos and prevailed. The universe was in darkness. *He* said, let there be light and let it prevail over darkness; and light came out of the womb of darkness and prevailed. *He* ordained the *Kali-Yug* — an age of darkness in which all Hind should lie at the feet of foreigners. And thus ye lie in the dust. But there is an end of night, and so there is an end to *Kali-Yug*. Bide ye the time, and watch!"

King drew me away, and we returned up-street between old temples and new iron-fronted stores toward Mulji Singh's quarters where he had left the traveling bag that we shared between us.

"Is that Gray Mahatma linked up with propaganda in the U.S.A?" I asked, wondering.

"What's more," King answered, "he's dangerous; he's sincere — the most dangerous type of politician in the world — the honest visionary, in love with an abstract theory, capable of offering himself for martyrdom. Watch him now!"

The crowd was beginning to close in on the Mahatma, seeking to touch him. Suddenly he flew into a fury, seized a long stick from some one near him and began beating them over the head, using both hands and laying on so savagely that ashes fell from him like pipe-clay from a shaken bag, and several men ran away with the blood pouring down their faces. However, they were reckoned fortunate.

"Some of those will charge money to let other fools touch them," said King. "Come on. Let's call on *her* now."

So we returned to Mulji Singh's stuffy little office, and King changed into a Major's uniform.

"It isn't exactly according to Hoyle to wear this," he explained. "However, she doesn't know I've resigned from the army."

CHAPTER II

THE PALACE OF YASMINI

Nobody saw us walk up to Yasmini's palace gate and knock; for whoever was abroad in the heat was down by the ghat admiring the Mahatma.

The bearded giant who had admitted us stood staring at King, his long, strong fingers twitching. In his own good time King turned and saw fit to recognize him.

"Oh, hullo Ismail!"

He held a hand out, but the savage flung arms about him that were as strong as the iron gate-clamps, and King had to fight to break free from the embrace.

"Now Allah be praised, he is father of mercies! *She* warned me!" he croaked. "She knows the smell of dawn at midnight! She said, 'He cometh soon!' and none believed her, save only I. This very dawn said she, 'Thou, Ismail,' she said, 'be asleep at the gate when he cometh and thine eyes shall be thrown to the city dogs!' Aye! Oho!"

King nodded to lead on, and Ismail obeyed with a deal of pantomime intended to convey a sense of partnership with roots in the past and its fruition now.

The way was down a passage between high, carved walls so old that antiquarians burn friendship in disputes not so much about the century as the very era of that quiet art — under dark arches with latticed windows into unexpected gardens fresh with the smell of sprinkled water — by ancient bronze gateways into other passages that opened into stone-paved courts with fountains in the midst — building joining on to building and court meeting court until, where an old black panther snarled at us between iron bars, an arch and a solid bronze door admitted us at last into the woman's pleasance — a wonderland of jasmine, magnolia and pomegranates set about a marble pool and therein mirrored among rainbow-colored fishes.

Beyond the pool a flight of marble steps rose fifty feet until it passed through a many-windowed wall into the *panch mahal* — the quarters of the women. At their foot Ismail halted.

"Go thou up alone! Leave this elephant with me!" he said, nudging me and pointing with his thumb toward a shady bower against the garden wall.

Without acknowledging that pleasantry King took my arm and we went straight forward together, our tread resounding strangely on steps that for centuries had felt no sterner shock than that of soft slippers and naked, jeweled feet.

We were taking nobody entirely by surprise; that much was obvious. Before we reached the top step two women opened a door and ran to meet us. One woman threw over King's head such a prodigious garland of jasmine buds that he had to loop it thrice about his shoulders. Then each took a hand of one of us and we entered between doors of many-colored wood, treading on mat-strewn marble, their bare feet pattering beside ours. There were rustlings to right and left, and once I heard laughter, smothered instantly.

At last, at the end of a wide hall before many-hued silken curtains our two guides stopped. As they released our hands, with the always surprising strength that is part of the dancing woman's stock-in-trade, they slipped behind us suddenly and thrust us forward through the curtains.

There was not much to see in front of us. We found ourselves in a paneled corridor, whose narrow windows overlooked the river, facing a painted door sixty paces distant at the farther end. King strode down the corridor and knocked.

The answer was one word that I did not catch, although it rang like a suddenly struck chord of music, and the door yielded to the pressure of King's hand.

I entered behind him and the door swung shut of its own weight with a click. We were in a high-ceilinged, very long room, having seven sides. There were windows to right and left. A deep divan piled with scented cushions occupied the whole length of one long wall, and there were several huge cushions on the floor against another wall. There was one other door besides that we had entered by.

We stood in that room alone, but I know that King felt as uneasy as I did, for there was sweat on the back of his neck. We were being watched by unseen eyes. There is no mistaking that sensation.

Suddenly a voice broke silence like a golden bell whose overtones go widening in rings into infinity, and a vision of loveliness parted the curtains of that other door.

"My lord comes as is meet — spurred, and ready to give new

kingdoms to his king! Oh, how my lord is welcome!" she said in Persian.

Her voice thrilled you, because of its perfect resonance, exactly in the middle of the note. She looked into King's eyes with challenging familiarity that made him smile, and then eyed me wonderingly. She glanced from me to a picture on the wall in blue of the Elephant-god — enormous, opulent, urbane, and then back again at me, and smiled very sweetly.

"So you have brought Ganesha with you? The god of good luck! How wonderful! How does one behave toward a real god?"

And while she said that she laid her hands on King's arms as naturally as if he were a lover whom she had not seen perhaps since yesterday. Plainly, there was absolutely nothing between him and her except his own obstinate independence. She was his if he wanted her.

She took King's hand with a laugh that had its roots in past companionship and led him to the middle, deepest window-seat, beneath which the river could be heard gurgling busily.

Then, when she had drawn the silken hangings until the softened light suggested lingering, uncounted hours, and had indicated with a nod to me a cushion in the corner, she came and lay on the cushions close to King, chin on hand, where she could watch his eyes.

King sat straight and square, watching her with caution that he did not trouble to conceal. She took his hand and raised the sleeve until the broad, gold, graven bracelet showed.

"That link forged in the past must bind us two more surely than an oath," she said smiling.

"I used it to show to the gatekeeper."

He sat cooly waiting for her next remark. And with almost unnecessary candor began to remove the bracelet and offer it back to her. So she unmasked her batteries, with a delicious little rippling laugh and a lazy, cat-like movement that betokened joy in the danger that was coming, if I know anything at all of what sign-language means.

"I knew that very day that you resigned your commission in the army, and I laughed with delight at the news, knowing that the gods who are our servants had contrived it. I know why thou art here," she said; and the change from you to thou was not haphazard.

"It is well known, Princess, that your spies are the cleverest in

India," King answered.

"Spies? I need no spies as long as old India lives. Friends are better."

"Do all princesses break their promises?" he countered, meeting her eyes steadily.

"Never yet did I break one promise, whether it was for good or evil."

"Princess," he answered, looking sternly at her, "in Jamrud Fort you agreed to take no part again in politics, national or international in return for a promise of personal freedom and permission to reside in India."

"My promise was dependent on my liberty. But is this liberty — to be forced to reside in this old palace, with the spies of the Government keeping watch on my doings, except when they chance to be outwitted? Nevertheless, I have kept my promise. Thou knowest me better than to think that I need to break promises in order to outwit a government of Englishmen!"

"Quibbles won't help, Princess," he answered. "You promised to do nothing that Government might object to."

"Well; will they object to my religion?" she retorted, mocking him. "Has the British *raj* at last screwed up its courage to the point of trespassing behind the purdah and blundering in among religious exercises?"

No man in his senses ever challenges a woman's argument until he knows the whole of it and has unmasked its ulterior purpose. So King sat still and said nothing, knowing that that was precisely what she did not want.

"You must make terms with me, heaven-born!" she went on, changing her tone to one of rather more suggestive firmness. "The *Kali-Yug* (age of darkness) is drawing to a close, and India awakes! There is froth on the surface — a rising here, an agitation there, a deal of wild talk everywhere, and the dead old government proposes to suppress it in the dead old ways, like men with paddles seeking to beat the waves down flat! But the winds of God blow, and the boat of the men with the paddles will be upset presently. Who then shall ride the storm? Their gunners will be told to shoot the froth as it forms and rises! But if there is a wise man anywhere he will make terms with me, and will set himself to guide the underlying forces that may otherwise whelm everything. I think thou art wise, my heaven-born. Thou wert wise once on a time."

"Do you think you can rule India?" King asked her; and he

did not make the mistake of suggesting ridicule.

"Who else can do it?" she retorted. "Do you think we come into the world to let fate be our master? Why have I royal blood and royal views, wealth, understanding and ambition, while the others have blindness and vague yearnings? Can you answer?"

"Princess," he answered, "I had only one object in coming here."

"I know that," she said nodding.

"I have simply come to warn you."

"*Chut!*" she answered with her chin between her hands and her elbows deep in the cushions. "I know how much is known. This man — what is his name? Ramsden? Pouff! Ganesha, here, is far better! Ganesha is from America. Those fools who went to prepare the American mind for what is coming, because they were altogether too foolish to be anything but in the way in India, have been found out, and Ganesha has come like a big bull-buffalo to save the world by thrusting his clumsy horns into things he does not understand! I tell you, Athelstan, that however much is known there is much more that is not known. You would better make terms with me!"

"What you must understand, Princess, is that your plan to overthrow the West and make the East the world's controlling force, is known by those who can prevent you," he answered quietly. "You see, I can't go away from here and tell whoever asks me that you are observing your promise to — — "

"No," she interrupted with a ringing merry laugh of triumph. "You speak truth without knowing it! You can not go away!"

Princess Yasmini's boast was good. But we had come to solve a problem, not to run away with it, and she looked disconcerted by our rather obvious willingness to be her prisoners for a while.

"Do you think I can not be cruel?" she asked suddenly.

"I have seen you at your worst, as well as at your best!" King answered.

"You act like a man who has resources. Yet you have none," she answered slowly, as if reviewing all the situation in her mind. "None knows where you are — not even Mulji Singh, with whom you left your other clothes before putting on that uniform the better to impress me! The bag that you and Ganesha share between you, like two mendicants emerging from the jail, is now in a room in this palace. You came because you saw that if I should be arrested there would be insurrection. You said so to Ommony sahib, and his butler overheard. But not even Ommony knows where you are. He said to you: 'If you can defeat that woman without using violence, you'll stand alone in the world as the one man who could do it. But if you use violence, though you kill her, she will defeat you and all the rest of us.' Is not that what your Friend Ommony said?"

"What kind of terms do you want me to make with you, Princess?" King answered.

"I can make you ruler of all India!" she said. "Another may wear the baubles, but thou shalt be the true king, even as thy name is! And behind thee, me, Yasmini, whispering wisdom and laughing to see the politicians strut!"

King leaned back and laughed at her.

"Do you really expect me to help you ruin my own countrymen, go back on my color, creed, education, oath and everything, and — — "

"Deluded fools! The East — the East, Athelstan, is waking! Better make terms with me, and thou shalt live to ride on the arising East as God rides on the wind and bits and governs it!"

"Very well," he said. "Show me. I'll do nothing blindfold."

"Hah! Thou art not half-conquered yet," she laughed. "And what of Ganesha? Is this mountain of bones and thews a person to be trusted, or shall we show him how much stronger than him is a horsehair in a clever woman's fingers?"

"This man Ramsden is my friend," King said.

"Are you *his* friend?" she retorted.

He nodded.

"You are going to see the naked heart of India!" she said. "Better to have your eyes burned out now than see that and be false to it afterward!"

Then, since we failed to order red-hot needles for our eyes, she cried out once — one clear note that sounded almost exactly as if she had struck a silver gong. A woman entered like the living echo to it. Yasmini spoke, and the woman disappeared again.

Below us the river swallowed and gurgled along the palace wall, and we caught the occasional thumping of a boat-pole. The thumping ceased exactly underneath us, and a man began singing in the time-hallowed language of Rajasthan. I think he was looking upward as he sang, for each word reached its goal.

"Oh warm and broad the plow land lies,

The idle oxen wait!
We pray thee, holy river, rise,
Nor glut thy fields too late!
The year awakes! The slumbering seed
Swells to its birth! Oh river, heed!"

"Strange time of year for that song, Princess! Is that one of your spies?" asked King, not too politely.

"One of my friends," she answered. "I told you: India awakes! But watch."

It was growing dark. Two women came and drew the curtains closer. Other women brought lamps and set them on stools along one wall; others again brought tapers and lit the candles in the hydra-headed candelabra.

"It is really too light yet," Yasmini grumbled, as if the gods who marshal in the night had not kept faith with her. But even so, the shadows danced among India's gods on the wall facing the row of stools.

Then there began wood-wind music, made by musicians out of sight, low and sweet, suggesting unimaginable mysteries, and one by one through the curtains opposite there came in silently seven women on bare feet that hardly touched the carpet; and all the stories about nautch girls, all the travelers' tales of how Eastern women dance with their arms, not feet, vanished that instant into the kingdom of lies. This was dancing — art absolute. They no longer seemed to be flesh and blood women possessed of weight and other limitations; their footfall was hardly audible, and you could not hear them breathe at all. They were like living shadows, and they danced the way the shadows of the branches do on a jungle clearing when a light breeze makes the trees laugh.

It had some sort of mystic meaning no doubt, although I did not understand it; but what I did understand was that the whole arrangement was designed to produce a sort of mesmerism in the beholder.

However, school yourself to live alone and think alone for a quarter of a century or so, meeting people only as man to man instead of like a sheep among a flock of sheep, and you become immune to that sort of thing.

The Princess Yasmini seemed to realize that neither King nor I were being drawn into the net of dreaminess that those trained women of hers were weaving.

"Watch!" said Yasmini suddenly. And then we saw what very few men have been priviliged to see.

She joined the dance; and you knew then who had taught those women. Theirs had been after all a mere interpretation: of her vision. Hers was the vision itself.

She was *It* — the thing itself — no more an interpretation than anything in nature is. Yasmini became India — India's heart; and I suppose that if King and I had understood her we would have been swept into her vortex, as it were, like drops of water into an ocean.

She was unrestrained by any need, or even willingness to explain herself. She was talking the same language that the nodding blossoms and the light and shadow talk that go chasing each other across the hillsides. And while you watched you seemed to know all sorts of things — secrets that disappeared from your mind a moment afterward.

She began singing presently, commencing on the middle F as every sound in nature does and disregarding conventional limitations just as she did when dancing. She sang first of the emptiness before the worlds were made. She sang of the birth of peoples; of the history of peoples.

She sang of India as the mother of all speech, song, race and knowledge; of truths that every great thinker since the world's beginning has propounded; and of India as the home of all of them, until, whether you would or not, at least you seemed to see the undeniable truth of that.

And then, in a weird, wild, melancholy minor key came the story of the *Kali-Yug* — the age of darkness creeping over India, condemning her for her sins. She sang of India under the hoof of ugliness and ignorance and plague, and yet of a few who kept the old light burning in secret — of hidden books, and of stuff that men call magic handed down the centuries from lip to lip in caves and temple cellars and mountain fastnesses, wherever the mysteries were safe from profane eyes.

And then the key changed again, striking that fundamental middle F that is the mother-note of all the voices of nature and, as Indians maintain, of the music of the spheres as well. Music and song and dance became laughter. Doubt vanished, for there seemed nothing left to doubt, as she began to sing of India rising at last, again triumphant over darkness, mother of the world and of all the nations of the world, awake, unconquerable.

Never was another song like that one! Nor was there ever such a climax. As she finished on a chord of triumph that seemed like a new spirit bursting the bonds of ancient mystery and sank to the floor among her women, there stood the Gray Mahatma in their midst, not naked any longer, but clothed from head to heel in a saffron-colored robe, and without his paste of ashes.

He stood like a statue with folded arms, his yellow eyes blazing and his look like a lion's; and how he had entered the room I confess I don't know to this hour, nor does Athelstan King, who is a trained observer of unusual happenings. Both doors were closed, and I will take oath that neither had been opened since the women entered.

"Peace!" was his first word, spoken like one in authority, who ordered peace and dared to do it.

He stood looking for more than a minute at King and me with, I think, just a flicker of scorn on his thin lips, as if he were wondering whether we were men enough to face the ordeal before us. Then indefinably, yet quite perceptibly his mood changed and his appearance with it. He held his right hand out.

"Will you not shake hands with me?" he asked smiling.

Now that was a thing that no sanctimonious Brahman would have dreamed of doing, for fear of being defiled by the touch of a casteless foreigner; so he was either above or below the caste laws, and it is common knowledge how those who are below caste cringe and toady. So he evidently reckoned himself above it, and the Indian who can do that has met and overcome more tyranny and terrors than the West knows anything about.

I wish I could make exactly clear what happened when I took his outstretched hand.

His fingers closed on mine with a grip like marble. There are few men who are stronger than I am; I can outlift a stage professional; yet I could no more move his hand or pull mine free than if he had been a bronze image with my hand set solid in the casting.

"That is for your own good," he said pleasantly, letting go at last. "That other man knows better, but you might have been so unwise as to try using violence."

"I'm glad you had that experience," said King in a low voice, as I went back to the window-seat. "Don't let yourself be bewildered by it. There's an explanation for everything. They know something that we don't, that's all."

CHAPTER III
FEAR IS DEATH

At a sign from the Gray Mahatma all the women except Yasmini left the room. Yasmini seemed to be in a strange mood mixed of mischief and amused anticipation.

The Mahatma sat down exactly in the middle of the carpet, and his method was unique. It looked just as if an unseen hand had taken him by the hair and lowered him gradually, for he crossed his legs and dropped to the floor as evenly and slowly as one of those freight elevators that disappear beneath the city sidewalks.

He seemed to attach a great deal of importance to his exact position and glanced repeatedly at the walls as if to make sure that he was not sitting an inch or two too far to the right or left; however, he had gauged his measurements exactly at the first attempt and did not move, once he was seated.

"You two *sahibs*," he began, with a slight emphasis on the word *sahib*, as if he wished to call attention to the fact that he was according us due courtesy, "you two honorable gentlemen," he continued, as if mere courtesy perhaps were not enough, "have been chosen unknown to yourselves. For there is but one Chooser, whose choice is never known until the hour comes. For the chosen there is no road back again. Even if you should prefer death, your death could not now be of your own choosing; for, having been chosen, there is no escape from service to the Purpose, and though you would certainly die if courage failed you, your death would be more terrible than life, since it would serve the Purpose without benefiting you.

"You are both honest men," he continued, "for the one has resigned honors and emoluments in the army for the sake of serving India; the other has accepted toilsome service under a man who seeks, however mistakenly, to serve the world. If you were not honest you would never have been chosen. If you had made no sacrifices of your own free will, you would not have been acceptable."

Yasmini clasped her hands and laid her chin on them among the cushions. She was reveling in intellectual enjoyment, as sinfully I daresay as some folk revel in more material delights. The

Mahatma took no notice of her, but continued.

"You have heard of the *Kali-Yug*, the age of darkness. It is at an end. The nations presently begin to beat swords into plowshares because the time has come. But there is yet much else to do, and the eyes of those who have lived so long in darkness are but blinded for the present by the light, so that guides are needed, who can see. You two shall see — a little!"

It was becoming intolerably hot in the room with the curtains drawn and all those lights burning, but I seemed to be the only one who minded it. The candles in the chandelier were kept from collapsing by metal sheaths, but the very flames seemed to feel the heat and to flicker like living things that wilted.

"Corn is corn and grass is grass," said the Mahatma, "and neither one can change the other. Yet the seed of grass that is selected can improve all grass, as they understand who strive with problems of the field. Therefore ye two, who have been chosen, shall be sent as the seeds of grass to the United States to carry on the work that no Indian can properly accomplish. Corn to corn, grass to grass. That is your destiny."

He paused, as if waiting for the sand to run out of an hour-glass. There was no hour-glass, but the suggestion was there just the same.

"Nevertheless," he went on presently, "there are some who fail their destiny, even as some chosen seeds refuse to sprout. You will need besides your honesty such courage as is committed to few.

"Once on a time before the *Kali-Yug* began, when the Aryans, of whom you people are descendants, lived in this ancient motherland, the whole of all knowledge was the heritage of every man, and what today are called miracles were understood as natural working of pure law. It was nothing in those days for a man to walk through fire unscathed, for there was very little difference between the gods and men, and men knew themselves for masters of the universe, subject only to *Parabrahm*.

"Nevertheless, the sons of men grew blind, mistaking the shadow for the substance. And because the least error when extended to infinity produces chaos, the whole world became chaos, full of nothing but rivalries, sickness, hate, confusion.

"Meanwhile, the sons of men, ever seeking the light they lost, have spread around the earth, ever mistaking the shadow for the substance, until they have imitated the very thunder and lightning, calling them cannon; they have imitated all the forces of the universe and called them steam, gasoline, electricity, chemistry and what not, so that now they fly by machinery, who once could fly without effort and without wings.

"And now they grow deathly weary, not understanding why. Now they hold councils, one nation with another, seeking to substitute a lesser evil for the greater.

"Once in every hundred years men have been sent forth to prove by public demonstration that there is a greater science than all that are called sciences. None knew when the end of the *Kali-Yug* might be, and it was thought that if men saw things they could not explain, perhaps they would turn and seek the true mastery of the universe. But what happened? You, who are from America; is there one village in all America where men do not speak of Indians as fakirs and mock-magicians? For that there are two reasons. One is that there are multitudes of Indians who are thieves and liars, who know nothing and seek to conceal their ignorance beneath a cloak of deceit and trickery. The other is, that men are so deep in delusion, that when they do see the unexplainable they seek to explain it away. Whereas the truth is that there are natural laws which, if understood by all, would at once make all men masters of the universe.

"I will give you an example. To-day they are using wireless telephones, who twenty years ago would have mocked whoever had suggested such a thing. Yet it is common knowledge that forty years ago, for instance, when Roberts the British general led an army into Afghanistan in wintertime and fought a battle at Kandahar, the news of his victory was known in Bombay, a thousand miles away, as soon as it had happened, whereas the Government, possessing semaphores and the telegraph, had to wait many days for the news.[1] How did that occur? Can you or any one explain it?

"If I were to go forth and tell how it happened, the men who profit by the telegraphs and the deep-sea cables, would desire to kill me.

"There is only one country in the world where such things

---

1   This is incontestably historical fact. See Lord Robert's book, *Forty-one Years in India.*

can be successfully explained, and that is India; but not even in India until India is free. When the millions of India once grasp the fact of freedom, they will forget superstition and understand. Then they will claim their powers and use them. Then the world will see, and wonder. And presently the world, too, will understand.

"Therefore, India must be free. These three hundred and fifty million people who speak one hundred and forty-seven languages must be set free to work out their own destiny.

"But there is only one way of doing that. The world, and India with it, is held in the grip of delusion. And what is delusion? Nothing but opinions. Therefore it is opinions that hold India in subjection, and opinions must be changed. A beginning must be made where opinions are least hidebound and are therefore easiest to change. That means America.

"Therefore you two *sahibs* are chosen — one who knows and loves India; one who knows and loves America. The duty laid on you is absolute. There can be no flinching from it. You are to go to America and convince Americans that India should be free to work out her own destiny.

"Therefore follow, and see what you shall see."

He rose, exactly as he had sat down, without apparent muscular effort. It was as if a hand had taken him by the scalp and lifted him, except that I noticed his feet were pressed so hard against the floor that the blood left them, so that I think the secret of the trick was perfect muscular control, although how to attain that is another matter.

The Princess Yasmini made no offer to come with us, but lounged among the cushions reveling in mischievous enjoyment. Whatever the Gray Mahatma's real motive, there was no possible doubt about hers; she was looking forward to a tangible, material profit.

The Gray Mahatma led the way through the door by which we had entered, stalking along in his saffron robe without the slightest effort to seem dignified or solemn.

"Keep your wits about you," King whispered; and then again, presently: "Don't be fooled into thinking that anything you see is supernatural. Remember that whatever you see is simply the result of something that they know and that we don't. Keep your hair on! We're going to see some wonderful stuff or I'm a Dutchman."

We passed down the long corridor outside Yasmini's room, but instead of continuing straight forward, the Gray Mahatma found an opening behind a curtain in a wall whose thickness could be only guessed. Inside the wall was a stairway six feet wide that descended to an echoing, unfurnished hall below after making two turns inside solid masonry.

The lower hall was dark, but he found his way without difficulty, picking up a lantern from a corner on his way and then opening a door that gave, underneath the outer marble stairway, on to the court where the pool and the flowering shrubs were. The lantern was not lighted when he picked it up. I did not see how he lighted it. It was an ordinary oil lantern, apparently, with a wire handle to carry it by, and after he had carried it for half a minute it seemed to burn brightly of its own accord. I called King's attention to it.

"I've seen that done before," he answered, but he did not say whether or not he understood the trick of it.

Ismail came running to meet us the instant we showed ourselves, but stopped when he saw the Mahatma and, kneeling, laid the palms of both hands on his forehead on the stone flags. That was a strange thing for a Moslem to do — especially toward a Hindu — but the Mahatma took not the slightest notice of him and walked straight past as if he had not been there. He could hear King's footsteps and mine behind him, of course, and did not need to look back, but there was something almost comical in the way he seemed to ignore our existence and go striding along alone as if on business bent. He acted as little like a priest or a fakir or a fanatic as any man I have ever seen, and no picture-gallery curator or theater usher ever did the honors of the show with less attention to his own importance.

He led the way through the same bronze gate that we had entered by and never paused or glanced behind him until he came to the cage where the old black panther snarled behind the bars; and then a remarkable thing happened.

At first the panther began running backward and forward, as the caged brutes usually do when they think they are going to be fed; for all his age he looked as full of fight as a newly caught young one, and his long yellow fangs flashed from under the curled lip — until the Mahatma spoke to him. He only said one word that I could hear, and I could not catch what the word was; but instantly the black brute slunk away to the corner of its cage farthest from the iron door, and at that the Mahatma opened the door without using any key that I detected. The padlock may have been a trick one, but I know this; — it came away in his hands the moment he touched it.

Then at last he took notice of King and me again. He stood aside, and smiled, and motioned to us with his hand to enter the cage ahead of him. I have been several sorts of rash idiot in my time, and I daresay that King has too, for most of us have been young once; but I have also hunted panthers, and so has King, and to walk unarmed or even with weapons — into a black panther's cage is something that calls, I should say, for inexperience. The more you know about panthers the less likely you are to do it. It was almost pitch-dark; you could see the brute's yellow eyes gleaming, but no other part of him now, because he matched the shadows perfectly; but, being a cat, he could see us, and the odds against a man who should walk into that cage were, as a rough guess, ten trillion to one.

"Fear is the presence of death, and death is delusion. Follow me then," said the Mahatma.

He walked straight in, keeping the lighted lantern on the side of him farthest from the panther, whose claws I could hear scratching on the stone flags.

"Keep that light toward him for God's sake!" I urged, having myself had to use a lantern more than a score of times for protection at night against the big cats.

"Nay, it troubles his eyes. For God's sake I will hide it from him," the Mahatma answered. "We must not wait here."

"Come on," said King, and strode in through the open door. So I went in too, because I did not care to let King see me hesitate. Curiosity had vanished. I was simply in a blue funk, and rather angry as well at the absurdity of what we were doing.

The Gray Mahatma turned and shut the gate behind me, taking no notice at all of the black brute that crouched in the other corner, grumbling and moaning rather than growling.

Have you ever seen a panther spit and spring when a keeper shoved it out of the way with the cleaning rake? There is no beast in the world with whom it is more dangerous to play tricks. Yet in that dark corner, with the lantern held purposely so that it should not dazzle the panther's eyes, the Gray Mahatma stirred the beast with his toe and drove him away as carelessly and incautiously as you might shove your favorite dog aside! The panther crowded itself against the side of the cage and slunk away behind us — to the front of the cage that is to say, close by the padlocked gate — where he crouched again and moaned.

The dark, rear end of the cage was all masonry and formed part of the building behind it. In the right-hand corner, almost invisible from outside, was a narrow door of thick teak that opened very readily when the Mahatma fumbled with it although I saw no lock, hasp or keyhole on the side toward us. We followed him through into a stone vault.

"And now there is need to be careful," he said, his voice booming and echoing along unseen corridors. "For though those here, who can harm you if they will, are without evil intention, nevertheless injury begets desire to injure. And do either of you know how to make acceptable explanations to a she-cobra whose young have been trodden on? Therefore walk with care, observing the lantern light and remembering that as long as you injure none, none will injure you."

At that he turned on his heel abruptly and walked forward, swinging the lantern so that its light swept to and fro. We were walking through the heart of masonry whose blocks were nearly black with age; there was a smell of ancient sepulchers, and in places the walls were damp enough to be green and slippery. Presently we came to the top of a flight of stone steps, each step being made of one enormous block and worn smooth by the sandalled traffic of centuries. It grew damper as we descended, and those great blocks were tricky things for a man in boots to walk on; yet the Gray Mahatma, swinging his lantern several steps below us, kept calling back:

"Have a care! Have a care! He who falls can do as much injury as he who jumps! Shall the injured inquire into reasons?"

We descended forty or fifty steps and I, walking last, had just reached the bottom, when something dashed between my feet, and another something flicked like a whip-lash after it. As the Mahatma swung the lantern I just caught sight of an enormous rat closely pursued by a six-foot snake, and after that we might as well have been in hell for all the difference it would have made to me.

I don't know how long that tunnel was, but I do know I am not going back there to measure it. It was nearly as big as the New York Subway, only built of huge stone blocks instead of concrete. It seemed to be an inferno, in which cobras hunted rats perpetually; but we saw one swarm of fiery-eyed rats eating a dead snake.

There were baby cobras by the hundred — savage, six-inch things, and even smaller, that knew as much of evil, and could slay as surely, as the full-grown mother-snake that raised her hood and hissed as we passed.

The snakes seemed afraid of the Mahatma, and yet not afraid of him — much more careful to keep out from under his feet than ours, yet taking no other apparent notice of him, whereas hundreds of them raised their hoods and hissed at us. And though nothing touched him, at least fifty times rats and snakes raced over King's feet and mine, or slipped between our legs.

"This fellow has some use for us," King said over his shoulder. "He'll neither be killed himself, nor let us be if he can help it. This is no new trick. Lots of 'em can manage snakes."

The Gray Mahatma, twenty yards ahead, heard every word of that. He stopped and let us come quite close up to him.

"Have you seen this?" he asked.

There was a cobra swinging its head about two and a half feet off the ground within a yard of him. He passed the lantern to me, and holding out both hands coaxed the venomous thing to come to him as you or I might coax a stray dog. It obeyed. It laid its head on his hands, lowered its hood, and climbed until, within six inches of his face, its head rested on his left shoulder.

"Would you like to try that?" he asked. "You can do it if you wish."

We did not wish, and while we stood there the infernal reptiles were swarming all around us, rising knee-high and swaying, with their forked tongues flashing in and out, but showing no inclination to use their fangs, although many of them raised their hoods. At that moment there were certainly fifty of the filthy things close enough to strike; and the bite of any one of them would have meant certain death within fifteen minutes.

However, they did not bite. The Gray Mahatma set down very gently the snake that had done his bidding, and then shooed the rest away; they backed off like a flock of foolish geese, hissing and swaying pretty much as geese do.

"Come!" he boomed. "Cobras are foolish people, and folly is infectious. Come away!"

CHAPTER IV

THE POOL OF TERRORS

We came soon to another flight of steps made of gigantic blocks of stone older than history, and groping our way up those we followed the Gray Mahatma to a gallery at the top, on the other side of which was a sheer drop and the smell of stagnant water. I could hear something sluggish that moved in the water, and somewhere in the distance was a turning around which light found its way so dimly that it hardly looked like light at all, but more like filmy mist. A heavy monster splashed somewhere beneath us and the Mahatma raised the lantern to peer into our faces.

"Those are *muggers* (alligators). You may see them now if you would rather. The same as with the snakes, the rule is you must do them no harm."

He looked at us keenly, as if making sure that we really were not enjoying ourselves, and then leaned his weight against an iron door in a corner. It swung open, and we followed him through into a pitch-dark chamber of some kind. But the door we came in by had hardly slammed behind us when a bright light broke through a square hole in the ceiling and displayed a flight of rock-hewn steps. Some one overhead had removed a stone plug from the hole.

The Mahatma motioned to King to go first, but as King refused he led the way again, going through the square hole overhead as handily as any seaman swinging himself into the cross-trees. King followed him and I stood on the top step with head and shoulders through the opening surveying the prospect before scrambling up after him.

I was looking between King's legs. The light came from three large wood-fires placed over at the left end of a rectangular chamber hewn out of solid rock. The chamber was at least a hundred feet long and thirty wide; its roof was lost in smoke, but seemed to be irregular, as if the walls of a natural cavern had been shaped by masons who left the high roof as they found it.

A very nearly naked man with a long beard, hair over his shoulders, and the general air of being some one in authority, was walking about with nothing in his hand except a seven-jointed bamboo cane. He was a very old man, but of magnificent physique and ribbed up like a race-horse in training. His principal business seemed to be the supervision of several absolutely naked individuals, who carried in wood through a dark gap in the wall and piled it on the three fires at the farther end with almost ludicrous precision.

And between the three fires, not spitted and not bound but absolutely motionless, there sat a human being, so dried out that not even that fierce heat could wring a drop of sweat from him, yet living, for you could see him breathe and the firelight shone on his living, yet unwinking eyes. Every draft of air that he drew into his lungs must have scorched him. Every single hair had disappeared from his body. And while we watched they came and fed him.

But he was only one of many, all undergoing torture in its most hideous and useless forms, and all as free as he was to deliver themselves if they saw fit. The least offensive was a man within six feet of me who sat on a conical stone no bigger than a cocoanut; that small stone was resting on top of a cone of rock about a yard high, in such fashion that it rocked at the slightest change of balance; the man's legs were crossed, however, exactly as if he were squatting on the floor — although they actually rested on nothing; and his arms had been crossed behind his back for so long, and held so steadily, that the fingernails of the right hand had grown through the left arm biceps, and vice versa. He, too, was fed with drops of water and about a dozen grains of rice — every second day, as the Mahatma told us afterward.

Space was at a premium in that gruesome madhouse. Close beside the fellow on the rocking stone there hung two ropes from rings in the roof. There were iron hooks on their lower ends, and these were passed through the back muscles of another naked man, who kept himself swinging by touching the floor with one toe. The muscles were so drawn by his weight that they formed loops several inches long and had turned to dry gristle; the strain had had some effect on one of his legs, for it was curled up under him and apparently useless, but the other, with which he toed the floor to swing himself, was apparently all right. His hands were folded over his breast, and his beard and hair hung like seaweed.

Near him again there was an arrangement like a medieval rack, only that instead of having a wheel or a lever the cords were drawn by heavy weights. A man lay on it with arms and legs stretched out toward its corners so tightly that his body did not touch the underlying strut; and he had been so long in that position that his hands and feet were dead from the pressure of the cords, and his limbs were stretched several inches beyond their normal length. In proof that his torture, too, was voluntary, he was balancing a round stone on his solar plexus that could have been much more easily dumped than kept in place.

The priest stared questioningly at the Gray Mahatma, glancing from him to us and back again.

The Gray Mahatma beckoned King and me and led the way between the shuddersome, self-immolated, twisted wrecks of humanity to an opening in the far wall, through which we passed into another chamber carved out of the rock, not so large as the first and only lighted by a charcoal brazier that gave off as much fumes as flame. The fitful, bluish light fell in a stone ledge, in a niche like a sepulcher, carved in one wall, and on that ledge a man lay who had every muscle of his body pierced with thorns; his tongue protruded between his teeth, and was held there by a thorn thrust through it.

The Gray Mahatma stood and looked at him, and smiled.

"Just a presumptuous fool!" he said pleasantly. "This was the most presumptuous of them all, but they all suffer for the same offense. Take warning! They could walk away if they cared to. They are here of what they think is their free will. They are moths who sought the flame, some from curiosity, some from desire, some craving adoration for themselves, all for one false reason or another. This fate might be yours — so take warning!

"There is not one of these who was not warned," he said quietly. "They were cautioned not to inquire into matters too deep for them. They were here to be taught; but that little knowledge that is such a dangerous thing tempted them too swiftly forward beyond their depth, so that now — you see them. They seek to get rid of material bodies and to satisfy themselves that death is a delusion. You revolt at the sight of these self-tortured fools; yet I tell you that, should you commit the same offense, you would behave as they, even as the moth that goes too near the flame. Take care lest curiosity overwhelm you."

"All right, lead along," King answered rather testily. "I've seen worse than this a hundred times. I've seen the women."

The Mahatma nodded gravely.

"But not even I may lead you forward clothed as you are," he said. "I am about to reveal such mysteries as set presumptuous fools to seeking perfection by a too short route. Even I would be slain, if I tried to introduce you in that garb. Undress."

He set us the example; but as we were not qualified by years of arduously won sanctity to stand stark naked in the presence he conceded us a clout apiece torn from a filthy length of calico that some one had tossed in a corner. And he tore another piece of filthy red cotton cloth in halves, and divided it between us to twist around our heads. King laughed at me.

"You look like a fine, fat Bengali," he said.

The Mahatma called to one of the servitors to bring ashes in a brass bowl. We watched him rake them out from under the fires, shake water on them, and mix them into paste as casually as if the business were part of his regular routine. The Mahatma took the bowl from him and plastered King and me liberally with the stuff, making King look like a scabrous fanatic, and I don't doubt I looked worse, having more acreage of anatomy. Last of all he put some on himself, but only here and there, as if his sanctity only demanded a little piercing out. Then he raised a flagstone in one corner of the chamber that swung easily on pivots set in sockets in the masonry, and led the way again.

We were evidently in a system of caves that had been quarried into shape centuries before the Christian era. They seemed originally to have been bubbles and blow-holes in volcanic rock, and to have been connected together by piercing the walls between them. There was certainly no intelligible plan attached to their arrangement, for we went first up, then down, then sideways, losing all sense of elevation and direction. But we passed through at least three score of those connected blow-holes, and the air in some of the higher ones was so foul that breathing it made you weak at the knees. Nevertheless, in every single one there was an anchorite of some kind, engaged in painful meditation. In each cave was an infinitesimal lamp made of baked clay and fed with vegetable oil that provided more smoke than flame, and the walls and ceiling were deep with the soot of centuries.

Following the Gray Mahatma's example King and I took handfuls of the soot and smeared it on our breasts, stomachs and faces, to mingle with the ashes in a mask of holiness. By the time we had finished that there was not much chance of any one mistaking us for anything but two half-crazed aspirants for sanctity.

I could not possibly have drawn a tracing of our own course, for it was rank bewildering; but we emerged at last under the stars by the side of a great stone tank. It might have been a bathing pool, for along each side steps disappeared into the water. We could dimly distinguish one end on our right hand with a row of great graven gods all reflected in the water; but the other end vanished through a black cave-mouth. It was about a hundred and twenty feet wide from bank to bank, and between us and the steps that faced us on the far side, in among the quivering star-reflections, I could count the snouts of eighteen alligators.

"Which way now?" King asked him a shade suspiciously.

"Forward," he answered, with a note of surprise.

But if the Mahatma supposed that a coat of soot and ashes provided either King or me with a satisfactory reason for hobnobbing with alligators in their home pool, he was emphatically mistaken. We objected simultaneously, unanimously, and right out loud in meeting.

"Suit yourself," said I. "This suits me here."

"Go forward if you like," said King, "we'll wait for you."

The Gray Mahatma turned and eyed us solemnly but not unkindly.

"If I should leave you here," he said, "a much worse fate would overtake you than any that you anticipate, for your minds are not advanced enough to imagine the horrors that assail all those who lack courage. This is the testing place for aspirants, and more win their way across it than you might suppose, impudence of ambition adding skill to recklessness. All must make the attempt, alone and at night, who seek the inner shrines of Knowledge, and those creatures in the tank have no other food than is thus provided.

"Those whose courage failed them are now such fakirs as we have seen, who now seek to rid themselves of materiality, which is the cause of fear, by ridding themselves of their fleshy envelope. Follow me then."

He stepped down into the water, and at once it became evident that to all intents and purposes there were two tanks, the division between them lying about eighteen inches under water. But the division was neither straight nor exactly level. It zigzagged this and that way like the key-track in a maze, and was more beset with slippery pitfalls than a mussel-shoal at low tide.

King followed the Mahatma in, and I came last, so I had the benefit of two pilots, as well as the important task of holding King whenever he groped his way forward with one foot. For the Mahatma went a great deal faster than we cared to follow, so that although he had shown us the way we were still doubtful of our footing. At intervals he would pause and turn and look at us, and every time he did that those long loathsome snouts would ripple toward him like spokes of a wheel, but he took no more notice of them than if they had been water-rats. They seemed more interested in him than in us.

There were seven sharp turns in that underwater causeway, and the edges of each turn were slippery slopes, up which an alligator certainly could climb, but that afforded not the least chance to a man whose foot once stepped too far and slid. And not only were there unexpected turns at different intervals, but there were gaps in the causeway of a yard or so in at least a dozen places, and the edges of those gaps were smooth and rounded, as if purposely designed to dump all wayfarers into the very jaws of the waiting reptiles. It was in just such places as that that they began to gather and wait patiently, with their awful yellow eyes just noticeable in the starlight.

King and I were standing on one such rounded guessing-place.

The Mahatma, twenty yards away, was taking his time about turning to give us directions, and one great fifteen foot brute had raised itself on the causeway behind us and was snapping its paws together like a pair of vicious castanets.

"Nero and Caligula were Christian gentlemen compared to you!" I called out to the Mahatma.

"You are fortunate," he boomed back. "You have starlight and a guide. Those who are not chosen have to find their way — or fail — alone under a cloudy sky. There is none to hold *them* while they grope; there is none to care whether they succeed or not, save only the *mugger* that desires a meal. Nevertheless, there are some of them who succeed, so how should you fail? Take a step to the left now — a long one, each holding the other, then another to the left — then to the right again."

"Curse you!" I shouted back, staring over King's shoulder. "There's a *mugger's* head between us and the next stepping-stone!"

"Nay!" he answered. "That *is* the stepping-stone."

I could have sworn that he was lying, but King set his foot on it and in a moment more we were working our way cautiously along the causeway again, making for the next sharp corner where the Mahatma had been standing to give us the direction. But he never waited for us to catch up with him. I think he suspected that in panic we might clutch him and offer violence, and he always moved on as we approached, leaving us to grope our way in agonies of apprehension.

The going did not become easier as we progressed. When the Gray Mahatma reached the steps on the far side and stood, out of the water waiting for us, all the monsters that had watched his progress came and joined our party; and now, instead of keeping to the water, two of them climbed up on the causeway, so that there was one of the creatures behind us and two in front.

"Call off your cousins and your uncles and your aunts!" I shouted, bearing in mind the Hindu creed that consigns the souls of unrighteous men to the bodies of animals in retribution for their sins.

The Gray Mahatma picked up a short pole from the embankment, and returned into the water with it, not striking out right and left as any ordinary-minded person would have done, but shoving the brutes away gently one by one, as if they were logs or small boats. And even so, they followed us so closely that they climbed the steps abreast of us.

But I'm willing to bet that there is not an alligator living that can catch me once my feet are set on hard ground, and I can say the same for King; we danced up those steps together like a pair of fauns emerging from a forest pool.

Then the Gray Mahatma came and peered into our faces, and asked an extraordinary question.

"Do you feel proud?" he asked, looking keenly from one to the other of us. "Because," he went on to explain, "you have now crossed the Pool of Terrors, and they are not so many who accomplish that. The *muggers* are well fed. And those who reach to this side are usually proud, believing they now have the secret key to the attainment of all Knowledge. You are going to see now what becomes of the proud ones."

The Mahatma led us forward toward a long, dark shadow that transformed itself into a temple wall as we drew closer, and in a moment we were once more groping our way downward amid prehistoric foundation stones, with bats flitting past us and a horrible feeling possessing me, at least, that the worst was yet to come.

The hunch proved accurate. We came into an enormous crypt that evidently underlay a temple. Great pillars of natural rock, practically square and twenty feet thick, supported the roof, which was partly of natural rock and partly of jointed masonry. There was nothing in the crypt itself, except one old gray-beard, who sat on a mat by a candle, reading a roll of manuscript; and he did not trouble to look up — did not take the slightest notice of us.

But around the crypt there were more cells than I could count off-hand. Some were dark. There were lights burning in the others. Each had an iron door with a few holes in it, and a small square window, unglazed and unbarred, cut in the natural rock. Enough light came through some of those square holes to suffuse the whole crypt dimly.

"None but an aspirant has ever entered here," said the Gray Mahatma. "Even when India was conquered, no enemy penetrated this place. You stand on forbidden ground."

He turned to the left and opened an iron cell door by simply pushing it; there did not seem to be any lock. He did not announce himself, but walked straight in, and we followed him. The cell was about ten feet by twelve, with a stone ledge wide enough to sleep on running along one side, and lighted by an oil lamp that hung by chains from the hewn roof. There were three bearded, middle-aged men, almost naked, squatting on one mat facing the stone ledge, one of whom held an ancient manuscript that all three were consulting; and on the stone ledge sat what once had been a man before those devils caught him.

The three looked up at the Gray Mahatma curiously, but did not challenge. I suppose his nakedness was his passport. They eyed King and me with a butcher's-eye appraisal, nodded, and resumed their consultation of the hand-written roll. The characters on it looked like Sanskrit.

The Gray Mahatma faced the creature on the stone ledge, and spoke to King and me in English.

"That," he said, "is one of those who crossed the Pool of Terrors and became insane with pride. Consider him. He entered here demanding knowledge, having only the desire and not the honesty. But since there is no way backward and even failure must subserve the universal cause, he was given knowledge and it made him what you see. Now these, who know a little and would learn more, make use of him as a subject for experiments.

"That thing, who was once a man, can imagine himself a bird, or a fish, or an animal — or even an insensate graven stone — at their command. When he is no more fit to be studied he will imagine himself to be a *mugger*, and will hurry into the tank with the other reptiles, and that will be the end of him. Come."

I felt like going mad that minute. I sat down on the rock floor and held my head to make sure that I still had it. I wanted to think of something that would give me back my grip on sanity and the good, clean concrete world outside; I don't think I could have done it if King had not seen and applied the solution. He kicked me in the ribs as hard as he could with his naked foot, and, that failing, used his fist.

"Get up!" he said. "Hit me, if you want to!"

Then he turned to the Mahatma.

"Confound you! Take us out of this!"

"Peace! Peace!" said the Gray Mahatma. "You are chosen. You are needed for another purpose. No harm shall come to either of you. There is one more cell that you must enter."

"No!" said I, and I met his eye squarely. "I've seen my fill of these sights. Lead the way out!"

He did not appear in the least afraid of me; merely curious, as if he were viewing an experiment. I made up my mind on the instant to experiment on my own account, and swung my fist back for a full-powered smash at him. I let go, too. But the blow fell on King, who stepped between us, and knocked nearly all the wind out of him.

"None o' that!" he gasped. "Let's see this through."

The Gray Mahatma patted him gently on the shoulder.

"Good!" he said. "Very good. You did well!"

CHAPTER V

FAR CITIES

The Gray Mahatma led the way toward one of the great square pillars that supported a portion of the roof.

In that pillar there was an opening, about six feet high and barely wide enough for a man of my build to squeeze himself through, but once inside it there was ample space and a stairway, hewn in the stone, wound upward. Still swinging the lantern he had brought with him from Yasmini's palace the Mahatma led the way up that, and we followed, I last as usual.

We emerged through a wooden door into a temple, whose walls were almost entirely hidden by enormous images of India's gods. There were no windows.

The resulting gloom was punctuated by dots of yellow light that came from hanging brass lamps, whose smoke in the course of centuries had covered everything with soot that it was nobody's business to remove. So it looked like a coal-black pantheon, and in the darkness you could hardly see the forms of long-robed men who were mumbling through some sort of ceremony.

"Those," said the Gray Mahatma, "are priests. They receive payment to pray for people who may not enter lest their sinfulness defile the sanctuary."

There was only one consideration that prevented me from looking for a door behind a carved stone screen placed at the end wall screen and bidding the Mahatma a discourteous farewell, and that was the prospect of walking through the streets with nothing on but a dish-rag and a small red turban.

However, the Gray Mahatma, as naked as the day he was born, led the way to the screen, opened a hinged door in it and beckoned us through; and we emerged, instead of into the street as I expected, into a marvelous courtyard bathed in moonlight, for the moon was just appearing over the roof of what looked like another temple at the rear.

All around the courtyard was a portico, supported by pillars of most wonderful workmanship; and the four walls within the portico were subdivided into open compartments, in each of which was the image of a different god. In front of each image hung a lighted lamp, whose rays were reflected in the idol's jeweled eyes; but the only people visible were three or four sleepy looking attendants in turbans and cotton loin-cloths, who sat up and stared at us without making any other sign of recognition.

In the very center of the courtyard was a big, square platform built of stone, with a roof like a canopy supported on carved pillars similar to those that supported the portico, which is to say that each one was different, and yet all were so alike as to blend into architectural harmony — repetition without monotony. The Gray Mahatma led the way up steps on to the platform, and waited for us at a square opening in the midst of its floor, beside which lay a stone that obviously fitted the hole exactly. There were no rings to lift the stone by from the outside, but there were holes drilled through it from side to side through which iron bolts could be passed from underneath.

Down that hole we went in single file again, the Gray Mahatma leading, treading an oval stairway interminably until I daresay we had descended more than a hundred feet. The air was warm, but breathable and there seemed to be plenty of it, as if some efficient means of artificial ventilation had been provided; nevertheless, it was nothing else than a cavern that we were exploring, and though there were traces of chisel and adze work on the walls, the only masonry was the steps.

We came to the bottom at last in an egg-shaped cave, in the center of which stood a rock, roughly hewn four-square; and on that rock, exactly in the middle, was a lingam of black polished marble, illuminated by a brass lamp hanging overhead. The Mahatma eyed it curiously:

"That," he said, "is the last symbol of ignorance. The remainder is knowledge."

There were doors on every side of that egg-shaped cave, each set cunningly into a natural fold of rock, so that they seemed to have been inset when it was molten, in the way that nuts are set into chocolate — pushed into place by a pair of titanic thumbs. And at last we seemed to have reached a place where the Gray Mahatma might not enter uninvited, for he selected one of the doors after a moment's thought and knocked.

We stood there for possibly ten minutes, without an answer, the Mahatma seeming satisfied with his own meditation, and we not caring to talk lest he should overhear us.

At last the door opened, not cautiously, but suddenly and wide, and a man stood square in it who filled it up from frame to frame — a big-eyed, muscular individual in loin-cloth and turban, who looked too proud to assert his pride. He stood with arms folded and a smile on his firm mouth; and the impression he conveyed was that of a master-craftsman, whose skill was his life, and whose craft was all he cared about.

He eyed the Mahatma without respect or flinching, and said nothing.

Have you ever watched two wild animals meet, stand looking at each other, and suddenly go off together without a sign of an explanation? That was what happened. The man in the doorway presently turned his back and led the way in.

The passage we entered was just exactly wide enough for me to pass along with elbows touching either wall. It was high; there was plenty of air in it; it was as scrupulously clean as a hospital ward. On either hand there were narrow wooden doors, spaced about twenty feet apart, every one of them closed; there were no bolts on the outside of the doors, and no keyholes, but I could not move them by shoving against them as I passed.

The extraordinary circumstance was the light. The whole passage was bathed in light, yet I could not detect where it came from. It was not dazzling like electricity. No one place seemed brighter than another, and there were no shadows.

The end of the passage forked at a perfect right angle, and there were doors at the end of each arm of the fork. Our guide turned to the right. He, King and the Mahatma passed through a door that seemed to open at the slightest touch, and the instant the Mahatma's back had passed the door-frame I found myself in darkness.

I had hung back a little, trying to make shadows with my hands to discover the direction of the light; and the strange part was that I could see bright light in front of me through the open door, but none of it came out into the passage.

It was intuition that caused me to pause at the threshold before following the others through. Something about the suddenness with which the light had ceased in the passage the moment the Mahatma's back was past the door, added to curiosity, made me stop and consider that plane where the light left off. Having no other instrument available, I took off my turban and flapped it to and fro, to see whether I could produce any effect on that astonishing dividing line, and for about the ten thousandth time in a somewhat strenuous career it was intuition and curiosity that saved me.

The instant the end of the turban touched the plane between light and darkness it caught fire; or rather, I should say fire caught it, and the fire was so intense and swift that it burned off that part of the turban without damaging the rest. In other words, there was a plane of unimaginably active heat between me and the rest of the party — of such extraordinary heat that it functioned only on that plane (for I could not feel it with my hand from an inch away); and I being in pitch darkness while they were in golden light, the others could not see me.

They could hear, however, and I called to King. I told him what happened, and then showed him, by throwing what was left of the turban toward him. It got exactly as far as the plane between light and darkness, and then vanished in a silent flash so swiftly and completely as to leave no visible charred fragment.

I could see all three men standing in line facing in my direction, hardly ten feet away, and it was difficult to remember that they could not see me at all — or at any rate that King could not; the others may have had some trained sixth sense that made it possible.

"Come forward!" said the Gray Mahatma. "We three came by. Why should it harm you?"

King sized up the situation instantly. If they intended to kill me and keep him alive, that would not be with his permission or connivance, and he stepped forward suddenly toward me.

"Stop!" commanded the Mahatma, showing the first trace of excitement that he had yet betrayed, but King kept on, and I suppose that the man who was acting showman did something, because King crossed the line without anything happening and then stood with one foot on each side of the threshold while I crossed.

"There are two of us in this!" he said to the Gray Mahatma then. "You can't kill one and take the other."

We were in a chamber roughly fifty feet square, whose irregular corners were proof enough that it had been originally another of those huge blow-holes in volcanic stone; the roof, too, had been left rough, but the greater part of the side-walls had been finished off smooth with the chisel, and hand-rubbed.

There was a big, rectangular rock exactly in the middle of the room, shaped like a table or an altar, and polished until it shone. I decided to sit down on it — whereat the Mahatma ceased to ignore me.

"Fool!" he barked. "Keep off that!"

I tore a piece off the rag I was wearing for a loin-cloth and tossed it on the polished surface of the stone. It vanished instantly and left no trace; it did not even leave a mark on the stone, and the burning was so swift and complete that there was no smell.

"Thanks!" I said. "But why your sudden anxiety on my account?"

He turned to King again.

"You have seen the *camera obscura* that shows in darkness the scenery near at hand, provided the sun is shining? The *camera obscura* is a feeble imitation of the true idea. There are no limits to the vision of him who understands true science. What city do you wish to see?"

"Benares," King answered.

Suddenly we were in darkness. Equally suddenly the whole top surface of the stone table became bathed in light of a different quality — light like daylight, that perhaps came upward from the stone, but if so came only a little way. To me it looked much more as if it began suddenly in mid-air and descended toward the surface of the stone.

And there all at once, as clearly as if we saw it on the focusing screen of a gigantic camera, lay Benares spread before us, with all its color, its sacred cattle in the streets, its crowds bathing in the Ganges, temples, domes, trees, movement — almost the smell of Benares was there, for the suggestion was all-inclusive.

"But why is it daylight in Benares while it's somewhere near midnight here?" King demanded.

That instant the sunshine in Benares ceased and the moon and stars came out. The glow of lamps shone forth from the temple courtyards, and down by the river ghats were the lurid crimson flame and smoke where they cremated dead Hindus. It was far more perfect than a motion picture. Allowing for scale it looked actually real.

Suddenly the chamber was all suffused in golden light once more and the picture on the granite table vanished.

"Name another city," said the Gray Mahatma.

"London," King answered.

The light went out, and there sure enough was London — first the Strand, crowded with motor-busses; then Ludgate Hill and St. Paul's; then the Royal Exchange and Bank of England;

then London Bridge and the Tower Bridge and a panorama of the Thames.

"Are you satisfied?" the Gray Mahatma asked, and once again the cavern was flooded with that peculiarly restful golden light, while the picture on the granite table disappeared.

"Not a bit," King answered. "It's a trick of some sort."

"Is wireless telegraphy a trick then?" retorted the Mahatma. "If so, then yes, so this is. Only this is as far in advance of wireless telegraphy, as telegraphy is in advance of the semaphore. This is a science beyond your knowledge, that is all. Name another city."

"Timbuctu," I said suddenly; and nothing happened.

"Mombasa," I said then, and Mombasa appeared instantly, with Kilindini harbor fringed with palm-trees.

I had been to Mombasa, whereas I never had seen Timbuctu. Almost certainly none present had ever seen the place, or even a picture of it.

The Gray Mahatma said something in a surly undertone and the golden light turned itself on again, flooding the whole chamber. King nodded to me.

"You can speak into a phonograph and reproduce your voice. There's no reason why you can't think and reproduce that too, if you know how," he said.

"Aye!" the Mahatma interrupted. "If you know how! India has always known how! India can teach these sciences to all the world when she comes into her freedom."

Throughout, the man who had admitted us had not spoken one word. He stood with arms folded, as upright as a soldier on parade. But now he unfolded his arms and began to exhibit signs of restlessness, as if he considered that the session had lasted long enough. However, he was still silent.

"Your honor is extremely clever. I've enjoyed the exhibition," I said to him in Hindustanee, but he took not the slightest notice of me, and if he understood he did not betray the fact.

"Let us go," said the Gray Mahatma, and proceeded to lead the way.

The Gray Mahatma took the other turning of the passage, and knocked on the door at the end. It was opened by a little man, who once had been extremely fat, for his skin hung about him in loose folds.

His cavern was smaller than the other, but as clean, and similarly flooded with the restful golden light. But he was only host;

the Gray Mahatma was showman. He said:

"All energy is vibrations; yet that is only one fraction of the truth. All is vibration. The universe consists of nothing else. Your Western scientists are just beginning to discover that, but they are men groping in the dark, who can feel but not see and understand. Throughout what all nations have agreed to call the dark ages there have been men called alchemists, whom other men have mocked because they sought to transmute baser metals into gold. Do you think they sought what was impossible? Nothing is impossible! They dimly discerned the possibility. And it may be that their ears had caught the legend of what has been known in India for countless ages.

"Gold is a system of vibrations, just as every other metal is, and the one can be changed into the other. But if you knew how to do it, would you dare? Can you conceive what would happen to the world if it were common knowledge, or even if it were known to a few, how the transmutation may be brought about? Now watch!"

What followed was convincing for the simple reason that there was nothing covered up, and no complicated apparatus that might cause you to suspect an ordinary conjuring trick. There were certainly strange looking boxes with hinged lids arranged on a ledge along one side of the chamber, but those were only brought into play when the funny little ex-fat man selected a lump of metal from them. On another ledge on the opposite side of the cell there were about a hundred rolls of very ancient-looking manuscripts, but he did not make use of them in any way.

The floor was bare, smooth rock; there was nothing on it, not even a mat. He laid a plain piece of wood on the floor and motioned us to be seated in front of it; so we squatted in a line with our backs to the door, King taking his place between the Mahatma and me. There was no hocus-pocus or flummery; the whole proceeding was as simple as playing dominoes.

Our host went to one of the peculiar looking boxes and selected a lump of what looked like lead. It was a small piece, about the size of an ordinary loaf of sugar and had no particular marks on it, except that it looked as if it might have been cut from a larger piece with shears or some such instrument. He dropped in into the middle of the slab of wood, and squatted in front of it, facing us, to watch.

I daresay it took twenty minutes for that lump of lead to

change into what looked like gold before our eyes. It began by sizzling, and melting in little pits and spots, but never once did the whole lump melt.

The tiny portions that melted and liquefied became full of motion, although the motion was never in one place for more than about a minute at a time; and wherever the motion had been the lump lost bulk, so that gradually the whole piece shrank and shrank. At the end it was not in its original shape, but had taken the form of a miniature cow's dropping.

I suppose it was hot. Our host waited several minutes before picking it off the slab.

At last he took the nugget off the slab and tossed it to King. King handed it to me. It was still warm and it looked and felt like gold. I laid it back on the slab.

"Do you understand it?" asked the Gray Mahatma.

CHAPTER VI

THE FIRE BATHERS

Our little wrinkly-skinned host did the honors as far as the door, and I thanked him for the demonstration; but the Gray Mahatma seemed displeased with that and ignoring me as usual, turned on King in the doorway almost savagely.

"Do you understand that whoever can do what you have just seen can also accomplish the reverse of it, and transmute gold into baser metal?" he demanded. "Does it occur to you what that would mean? A new species of warfare! One combination of ambitious fools making gold — another unmaking it. Chaos! Now you shall see another science that is no fit pabulum for fools."

We came to a door on our right. It was opened instantly by a lean, mean-looking ascetic, whose hooked nose suggested an infernal brand of contempt for whoever might not agree with him. Just as the others had done, he met the Gray Mahatma's eyes in silence, and admitted us by simply turning his back. But this door only opened into another passage, and we had to follow him for fifty feet and then through another door into a cavern that was bigger than any. And this time our host was not alone. We were expected by a dozen lean, bronze men, who squatted in a row on one mat with expressionless faces. They were not wearing masks, but they looked as if they might have been.

This last cavern was certainly a blow-hole. Its round roof, blackened with smoke, was like the underside of a cathedral dome. No effort seemed to have been made to trim the walls, and the floor, too, had been left as nature made it, shaped something like a hollow dish by the pressure of expanding gases millions of years ago when the rock was molten.

The very center of the vast floor was the lowest point of all, and some work had been done there, for it was shaped into a rectangular trough thirty feet long by ten wide. That trough — there was no guessing how deep it might be — was filled almost to the brim with white-hot charcoal, so that obviously there was a means of forcing a draft into it from underneath.

"Now," said the Mahatma, turning to King as usual and ignoring me, "your friend may submit to the test if he wishes. He may walk on that furnace. He shall walk unscathed. I promise it."

King turned to me.

"What d'you say?" he asked. "I've seen this done before.[2] It can be done. Shall we try it together?"

I did not hesitate. There are times when even such a slow thinker as I am can make up his mind in a flash. I said "No" with such emphasis that King laughed. The Mahatma looked at me rather pityingly, but made no comment. He invited the two of us to sit down, so we squatted on the floor as close to the trough as we could go without being scorched. There were no screens or obstructions of any kind, and the only appliance in evidence was an iron paddle, which the man who had admitted us picked up off the floor.

He took that paddle, and without any preliminary fuss or hesitation walked straight on to the bed of white-hot charcoal, beginning at one end, and smoothed the whole glowing surface with the paddle, taking his time about it and working with as little excitement as a gardener using a rake. When he had finished the end of the paddle was better than red-hot — a good cherry-red.

The hairs on his legs were unscorched. The cotton cloth of which his kilt was made showed not the slightest trace of burning.

As soon as he had sat down the other twelve advanced toward the fire. Unlike him, they were stark naked. One by one they walked into the fire and traversed it from end to end with no more sign of nervousness than if they had been utterly unconscious of its existence. Then they turned around and walked back again.

"Is it the men or the fire?" King demanded.

"Neither," the Mahatma answered. "It is simply knowledge. Any one can do it, who knows how."

One of the men approached the fire again. He sat down on it, and went through the motions of bathing himself in the white-hot flame, turning his head repeatedly to grin at us. Then, lying down full-length, he rolled from end to end of the furnace, and walked away at last as casually as if he had come out of a bath. It was perfectly astonishing stuff to watch.

"If this isn't superstition, or mesmerism, or deception of

2   See the newspaper accounts of fire-walking in the presence of the Prince of Wales and about a thousand witnesses mostly European.

some kind, why do you insist on all this mummery of soot and ashes for my friend and me?" King demanded. "Why do you use a temple full of Hindu idols to conceal your science, if it is a natural science and not trickery?"

The Gray Mahatma smiled tolerantly.

"Can you suggest a better way of keeping the secret?" he answered. "We are protected by the superstition. Not even the Government of India would dare arouse the superstitious wrath of a people by inquiring too closely into what goes on beneath a temple. If we were to admit that what we know is science, just as wireless telegraphy is a science, we would not be safe for an hour; the military, the kings of commerce, the merely curious, and all the enemies of mankind would invent ten thousand excuses of investigating us."

"Where did you learn English?" King demanded.

"I am a Ph.D. of Johns Hopkins," the Gray Mahatma answered. "I have traveled all over the United States seeking for one man who might be trusted with the rudiments of our science. But I found none."

"Suppose you had found the wrong man — and trusted him?" King suggested.

"My friend," said the Gray Mahatma, "you are better known to us than we to you. You are a man incapable of treachery. You love India, and all your life you have striven to act always and in all things like a man. You have been watched for years. Your character has been studied. If our purpose had been to conquer the world, or to destroy the world, we would never have selected you. There is no need to speak to you of what would happen if you should commit treachery. There is no risk of your explaining the secret of our science to the wrong individual, for you are not going to be taught it."

"Well, what of my friend Ramsden?" King asked him.

"Your friend Mr. Ramsden, I think, will never again see the United States."

"Why?"

"He has seen too much for his own good. He lacks your mentality. He has bravery of a kind, and honesty of a kind; but he is — not — the right — man — for — our — purpose. He made a mistake when he came with you."

King looked straight into the eyes of the Gray Mahatma.

"You think you know me?" he asked.

"I know you better than you know yourself!"

"That's possible," said King. "Do you suppose I would tell you the truth?"

"I know it. I am sure of it. You have too much integrity to deal in lies."

"Very well," King answered quietly, "it's both of us or neither. Either we both go free, or you do your worst to us both. This man is my friend."

The Gray Mahatma smiled, and thought, and smiled, and looked at King, and then away again.

"It would be a pity to destroy yourself," he said at last. "Nevertheless, you are the only chance your friend has. I have no enmity against him; he is merely unsuitable; he will be the victim of his own shortcomings, unless you can rescue him. But if you make the attempt and fail, I am afraid, my friend, that that will be the end of both of you."

It was rather like listening to your own autopsy! I confess that I began again to feel horribly afraid, although not so much so that I cared to force King into danger on my account, and once more I made my mind up swiftly. I reached out to seize the Gray Mahatma by the throat. But King struck my hand up.

"We're two to their many," he said sternly. "Keep your hair on!"

The Mahatma smiled and nodded.

"A second time you have done well," he exclaimed. "If you can keep the buffalo from blundering — but we waste time. Come."

King put his hands on my shoulders, and we lock-stepped out of the cavern behind the Mahatma, looking, I don't doubt, supremely ridiculous, and I for one feeling furiously helpless.

We entered another cave, whose dome looked like an absolutely perfect hemisphere, but the whole place was so full of noise that your brain reeled in confusion. There were ten men in there, naked to the waist as all the rest had been, and every single one of them had the intelligent look of an alert bird with its head to one side. They were sitting on mats on the floor in no apparent order, and each man had a row of tuning forks in front of him, pretty much like any other tuning forks, except that there were eight of them to each note and its subdivisions.

Every few minutes one of them would select a fork, strike it, and listen; then he would get up, dragging his mat after him with all the forks arranged on it, and sit down somewhere else. But the tuning forks were not the cause of the din. It was the roar of a great city that was echoing under the dome — clatter of traffic and men's voices, whistling of the wind through overhead wires, dogs' barking, an occasional bell, at intervals the whistle of a locomotive and the rumble and bump of a railroad train, whirring of dynamoes, the clash and thump of trolley cars, street-hawkers' cries, and the sound of sea-waves breaking on the shore.

"You hear Bombay," said the Mahatma. Then we all sat down in line.

It was actual physical torture until you were used to it, and I doubt whether you could get used to it without somebody to educate you — some scientist to show you how to defend your nerves against that outrageous racket. For the sounds were all out of adjustment and proportion. Nothing was in key. It was as if the laws of acoustics had been lifted, and sound had gone crazy.

At one moment, apropos of nothing and disconnected from all other sounds, you could hear a man or a woman speaking as distinctly as if the individual were up there under the dome; then a chaos of off-key notes would swallow the voice, and the next might be a dog's bark or a locomotive whistle. The only continuously recognizable sounds were a power station and the thunder of waves along the harbor front, and it sounded much more thunderous than it should have done at that season of the year.

The tuning of an orchestra does not nearly approximate the confusion; for the members of the orchestra are all trying to find one pitch and are gradually hitting it, whereas every sound within that cavern seemed to be pitched and keyed differently.

"This is our latest," said the Mahatma. "It is only for two or three hundred years that we have been studying this phenomenon. It may possibly take us two or three hundred years more before we can control it."

I wanted to ask questions, but could not because the cursed inharmony made my senses reel. Nevertheless, you could hear other sounds perfectly. When I struck my hand on the rock floor I could hear the slap at least as distinctly as normal; possibly a little more so. And when the Gray Mahatma spoke, each word was separate and sharp.

"Now you shall hear another city," he said. "Observe that the voices of cities are as various as men's. No two are alike. Sound and color are one and the same thing differently expressed, and the graduations of both are infinite."

He caught the eye of one of the men.

"Calcutta!" he said, in a voice not exactly of command, yet certainly not of deference.

Without acknowledging the order in any other way, the man got on his knees and picked up an enormous tuning fork, whose prongs were about three feet long, and he made some adjustment in the fork of it that took about five minutes. He might have been turning the screw of a micrometer; I could not see. Then, raising the fork above his shoulder, he struck the floor with it, and a master-note as clear as the peal of a bell went ringing up into the dome.

The effect was almost ridiculous. It made you want to laugh. Everybody in the cavern smiled, and I daresay if the truth were known we had discovered the mother-lode of comedy. That one note chased all the others out of the dome as a dog might chase sheep — as the wind blows clouds away — as a cop drives small boys off the grass. They actually scampered out of hearing, and you couldn't imagine them hiding close by, either; they were gone for good, and that one, clear master-note — the middle F — went vibrating around and around, as if scouring out the very smell of what had been there.

"That is the key-note of all nature," said the Mahatma. "All sounds, all colors, all thoughts, all vibrations center in that note. It is the key that can unlock them all."

The silence that followed when the last ringing overtone had gone off galloping in its stride toward infinity was the most absolute and awful silence I have ever had to listen to. The very possibility of sound seemed to have ceased to exist. You could not believe that there could be sound, nor remember what sound was like. A whole sense and its functions had been taken from you, and the resultant void was dead — so dead that no sense could live in it, unless fear is a sense. You could feel horribly afraid, and I'll tell you what the fear amounted to:

There was a feeling that these men were fooling with the force that runs the universe, and that the next stroke might be a mistake that would result like the touching of two high-tension wires, multiplied to the *nth*. You could not resist the suggestion that the world might burst in fragments at any minute.

Meanwhile the fellow with the tuning fork fiddled again with some adjustment on the thick portion of its stem, and presently whirling it around his head as the old-time warriors used two-handed swords, he brought it down on one of a circle of small anvils that were arranged around him like the figures on a clock-face.

You could almost see Calcutta instantly! The miracle was the reverse of the preceding one. The ringing, subdivided, sharp, discordant note he struck was swallowed instantly in a sea of noise that seemed not only to have color but even smell to it; you could smell Calcutta! But that, of course, was mere suggestion — a trick of the senses of the sort that makes your mouth water when you see another fellow suck a lemon.

You could even hear the crows that sit on the trees in the park and caw at passers-by. You could hear the organ in a Christian church, and the snarl of a pious Moslem reading from the Koran. There was the click of ponies' hoofs, the whirring and honk of motor-cars, the sucking of Hoogli River, booming of a steamer-whistle, roars of trains, and the peculiar clamor of Calcutta's swarms that I can never hear without thinking of a cobra with its hood just ready to raise.

In the sea of noises in the dome one instantly stood out — the voice of a man speaking English with a slightly babu accent. For exactly as long as the reverberations of those two tuning forks lasted, you could hear him declaiming, and then his voice faded away into the ocean of noise like a rock that has shown for a moment above the surface of a maelstrom.

"That is a member of the legislature, where ignorant men in all-night session make laws for fools to break," said the Gray Mahatma.

Signing to King and me to remain seated, he himself crossed the floor to where the master-tuner sat, and squatting down beside him began picking up tuning forks and striking one against the other. Each time he did that some city sound or other distinguished itself for a moment, exactly as the theme appears in music; only some of the vibrations seemed to jar against others instead of blending with them, and when that happened the effect was intensely disagreeable.

At last he struck a combination that made me jump as effectually as sudden tooth-ache. Some of the other sounds had affected King more, but that particular one passed him by and tortured me. Watching with his head a little to one side the Gray Mahatma instantly began striking those two forks as rapidly as if he were clapping hands, increasing the vehemence with each stroke.

If I had stayed there I would have been stark mad or dead within five minutes. I felt as if I were being vibrated asunder — as if my whole body were resolving into its component parts. I lay on the floor with my head in both hands, and I daresay yelled with agony, but I don't know about that.

At any rate King understood and acted instantly. He seized me under the arms and dragged me face-downward to the door, where he had to drop me in order to find how to open the thing. Having accomplished that, he dragged me through into the passage, where the agony ceased as instantly as the ache does when a dentist pulls an abscessed tooth. No one sound reached us through the open door. However immature that particular branch of their science might be, they had learned the way of absolutely localizing noise.

The Gray Mahatma came out smiling, and ignoring me as if I was not there.

He opened another door, not requiring to knock this time, and led the way along another passage that wound through solid rock for what can hardly have been less than a quarter of a mile.

King had dragged me out of that dome of dins in the nick of time, and my head was recovering rapidly. By the time we reached a door at the end of that long passage I could think clearly, and although too weak to stand upright without holding on to something, was sufficiently recovered to know that the remainder would be only a matter of minutes. And we spent three or four of the minutes waiting for the door to open, which it did at last suddenly.

A man appeared in the opening, whose absolutely white hair reached below his shoulder-blades, and whose equally white beard descended to his middle. He wore the usual loin-cloth, but was usual in nothing else. He looked older than Methuselah, yet strong, for his muscles stood out like knotted whip-cords; and active, for he stood on the balls of his feet with the immobility that only comes of ableness. The most unusual thing of all was that he spoke. He said several words in Sanskrit to the Gray Mahatma, before turning his back on us and leading the way in.

CHAPTER VII

MAGIC

We went into a cavern whose floor was cup-shaped. Nearly all the way around the rim of the cup was an irregular ledge averaging twenty feet in width; with that exception, the whole interior was shaped like an enormous egg with its narrow end upward. The bottom was nowhere less than a hundred feet across, and was reached by steps cut irregularly downward from the rim.

At intervals around the ledge were seated about a score of men, some solitary, some in groups of three; some were naked, others wore loin-cloths; all were silent, but they all took an obvious interest in us, and some of them were grinning. A few of them squatted, with their legs tucked under them, but most of them let their legs hang over the edge, and they all had an air of perfect familiarity with the surroundings as well as what can be best described as a "team look." You see the same air of careless competence around a well-managed circus lot.

King and I followed the Gray Mahatma down into the bowl, and under his directions seated ourselves exactly in the middle, King and I back to back and the Mahatma a little way from us and also with his back turned. In that position my back was toward the door we had entered by, but I was able to see nine narrow openings in the opposite wall about twenty feet higher than the ledge, and those openings may have had something to do with what followed, although I can't prove it.

Old gray-beard, who had admitted us, stood on the ledge like a picture of St. Simon Stylites, folding his arms under his flowing beard and looking almost ready to plunge downward, as if the bowl were a swimming tank.

However, he suddenly filled his great scrawny breast with air and boomed out one word. The golden light ceased to exist. There was no period of going, as there is even with electric light. He spoke, and it was not. Nothing whatever was visible. I held a finger up, and poked my eye before I knew it.

Then all at once there began the most delicious music, like Ariel singing in mid-air. It was subdued, but as clear as the ripple of a mountain stream over pebbles, and there was absolutely no locating it, for it seemed to come from everywhere at once, even from underneath us. And simultaneously with the music there began to be a dim light, which was all the more impossible to locate because it was never the same color in two places, nor even in one place for longer than a note of music lasted.

"Observe!" boomed the Gray Mahatma's solemn voice. "Color and sound are one. Both are vibration. You shall behold the color harmonies."

Presently the connection between sound and color began to be obvious. Each note had its color, and as that note was sounded the color appeared in a thousand places.

It was Eastern music. It filled the cavern, and as the pulse of it quickened the light danced, colors shooting this and that way like shuttles weaving a new sky. But there were no drum-beats yet, and the general effect was rather of dreaminess.

When the old gray-beard's voice boomed out at last from the ledge above us, and light and music ceased simultaneously, the effect was nauseating. It went to the pit of your stomach. The instantaneous darkness produced vertigo. You felt as if you were falling down an endless pit, and King and I clutched each other. The mere fact that we were squatting on a hard floor did not help matters, for the floor seemed to be falling too and to be turning around bewilderingly, just as the whorls of colored light had done. The gray-beard's voice boomed again; whereat there was more music, and light in tune to it.

This time, of all unexpected things, Beethoven's Overture to Leonore began to take visible form in the night, and I would rather be able to set down what we saw than write Homer's Iliad! It must be that we knew then all that Beethoven did. It was not just wind music, or mere strings, but a whole, full-volumed orchestra — where or whence there was no guessing; the music came at you from everywhere at once, and with it light, interpreting the music.

To me that has always been the most wonderful overture in the world anyhow, for it seems to describe creation when the worlds took form in the void; but with that light, each tone and semi-tone and chord and harmony expressed in the absolutely pure color that belonged to it, it was utterly beyond the scope of words. It was a new unearthly language, more like a glimpse of the next world than anything in this.

The combination of color and music was having a highly desirable effect on me. Nothing could have done more to counteract the effects of the godless din that bowled me over in the other cavern.

But King was having a rotten time. He was heaving now as he tried to master himself. I heard him exclaiming —

"Oh my God!" as if the physical torture were unbearable.

The Gray Mahatma was not troubling about King. He had shifted his position so as to watch me, and he seemed to expect me to collapse. So I showed as little as possible of my real feelings, and shut my eyes at intervals as if bewildered. Then he cried out just as the gray-beard on the ledge had done.

The overture to Leonore ceased. The colors gave place to the restful golden light. King had not collapsed yet, and his usual Spartan self-mastery prevented him then from betraying much in the way of symptoms. So I clutched my head and tried to look all-in, which gave me a chance to whisper to King under my arm.

"Can you hang on?"

"Dunno. How are you doing?"

"Fine."

The Gray Mahatma seemed to think that I was appealing to King for help. He looked delighted. Between my fingers I could see him signaling to the gray-beard on the ledge. The golden light vanished again. And now once more they gave us Eastern music, awful stuff, pulsating with a distant drumbeat like the tramp of an army of devils. The colors were angry and glowering now. The shapes they took as they plaited and wove themselves into one another were all involuted, everything turning itself inside out, and the end of every separate movement was blood-red.

King groaned aloud and rolled over on his side, just as the stuff became so dim and dreadful that you could hardly see your hand before your face, and a noise like the rushing of the wind between the worlds made every inch of your skin prickly with goose-flesh. Low though the colors were, when you shut your eyes you could still see them, but I could not see the Gray Mahatma, and I was sure he could not see me. He would not know which of us was down and out.

So I seized King and dragged him across the floor to the point where the irregular stone steps provided the only way of escape. There I hove him like a sack on to my shoulders. In that drunken, throbbing twilight it would have been easy for some of the gray-beard's crew to lean from the ledge and send me reeling back again; the best chance was to climb quickly before they were aware of me.

When I reached the ledge it was deserted. There was nothing whatever to indicate where the gray-beard and his crew were. I could not remember exactly the direction of the entrance, but made for the wall, intending to feel my way along it; and just as I started to do that I heard the Gray Mahatma climbing up behind me.

He made hardly more noise than a cat. But though the Mahatma was stealthy, he came swiftly, and in a moment I felt his hand touch me. That was exactly at the moment when the music and colors were subdued to a sort of hell-brew twilight — the kind of glow you might expect before the overwhelming of the world.

"You are as strong as the buffalo himself," he said, mistaking me for King. "Leave that fool here, and come with me."

My right hand was free, but the Gray Mahatma had plenty of assistance at his beck and call.

So I put my hand in the small of his back and shoved him along in front of me. If he should learn too soon that King, and not I, was down and out he might decide to have done with us both there and then. My task was to get out of that cavern before the golden light came on again.

The Gray Mahatma led the way to the door, and it was just as well that he did, for there was some secret way of opening it that I should almost certainly have failed to find. I pushed him through ahead of me.

And then we were in pitch darkness. There was neither light, nor room to turn, and nothing for it but for the Mahatma to lead the way along, and I had to be careful in carrying King not to injure him against the rock in the places where the passage narrowed.

However, he began to recover gradually as we neared the end of the long passage, regaining consciousness by fits and starts like a man coming out of anesthesia, and commencing to kick so that I had hard work to preserve him from injury. When his feet were not striking out against the walls his head was, and I finally shook him violently. That had the desired effect. It was just as if fumes had gone out of his head. His body grew warmer almost in a moment, and I felt him break out into a sweat. Then he groaned, and asked me where we were; and a moment later he seemed to understand what was happening, for he struggled to free himself.

"All right," he whispered. "Let me walk."

So I let him slip down to his feet in front of me, and holding him beneath the armpits repeated our lock-step trick with positions reversed; and when we reached the outer door that gave on to the narrow main passage he was going fairly strong. The Mahatma opened the door and stepped out into the light; but it was the strange peculiarity of that light that it did not flow beyond its appointed boundaries, and we continued to be in darkness as long as we did not follow him through the door.

So when King stepped out ahead of me, the Mahatma had no means of knowing what a mistake he had been making all along. He naturally jumped to the conclusion that King had been carrying me.

When I stepped out of the pitch blackness he looked more than a little surprised at my appearance, and I grinned back at him as sheepishly as I could manage, hoping he would not see the red patch on my shoulder caused by the pressure of King's weight, or the scratches made by King's fingernails when he was beginning to recover consciousness. Nevertheless, he did see, and understood.

"Lead on, MacDuff!" I said in plain English, and perhaps he did not dislike me so immensely after all, for he smiled as he turned his back to lead the way.

We passed, without meeting anybody, out through the narrow door where the first tall speechless showman had admitted us, into the cave where the lingam reposed on its stone altar; and there the Mahatma resumed the lantern he had left.

When we climbed the oval stairway and emerged on the platform under the cupola the dawn was just about to break. The Gray Mahatma raised the stone lid with an ease that betrayed unsuspected strength and dropped it into place, where it fitted so exactly that no one ignorant of the secret would ever have guessed the existence of a hidden stairway.

Swinging his lantern the Mahatma led into the temple, where the enormous idols loomed in quivering shadow, and made straight for the biggest one of all — the four-headed one that faced the marble screen. I thought he was going to bow down and worship it. He actually did go down on hands and knees, and I turned to King in amazement, thus missing my chance to see what he was really up to.

So I don't know how he managed it; but suddenly the whole lower part of the idol, including the thighs, swung outward and disclosed a dark passage, into which he led us, and the stone swung back into place at our backs as if balanced by weights.

At the far end the Mahatma led into a square-mouthed tunnel, darker if that were possible than the vaulted gloom we had left, and as we entered in single file I thought I heard the splashing of water underneath.

About a minute after that the Mahatma stopped and let King draw abreast; then, continuing to swing the lantern he started forward again. I don't know whether it was fear, intuition, or just curiosity that made me wonder why he should change the formation in that way, but quite absurdly I deduced that he wished King to walk into a trap. It was that that saved me.

"Look out, King!" I warned.

Exactly as I spoke I set my foot on a yielding stone trapdoor — felt a blast of cool air — and heard water unmistakably. The air brought a stagnant smell with it. I slid forward and downward, but sprang simultaneously, managing to get my fingers on the edge of the stone in front. But the balanced trapdoor, resuming its equilibrium, caught me on the back of the head, half-stunning me, and in another second I would have gone down into the dark among the alligators. I just had enough consciousness left to realize that I was hanging over the covered end of the alligator tank.

But the faint outer circle of light cast by the Mahatma's lantern just reached me, and as King turned his head to acknowledge my warning he saw me fall. He sprang back, and seized my wrists, just as my fingers began slipping on the smooth stone; but my weight was almost too much for him, and I came so near to dragging him through after me that the stone trap got past my head and jammed against my elbows.

Then I heard King yelling for the Mahatma to bring the lantern back, and after what seemed an interminable interval the Mahatma came and set one foot on the stone, so that it swung past my head again, nearly braining me in its descent. I don't know whether he intended that or not.

"There is more in this than accident," he said, his voice booming hollow as he bent to let the light fall on me. "Very well; pull up your buffalo, and you shall have him!"

It was no easy task for the two of them to haul me up, because the moment the Mahatma removed his foot from the lid of the trap the thing swung upward and acted like the tongue of a buckle to keep me from coming through. When he set his foot on it again, the other foot did not give him sufficient purchase. Finally King managed to pull his loin-cloth off and pass it around under my armpits, after which the two together hauled me clear, minus in the aggregate about a half square foot of skin that I left on the edge of the stone.

Off the Mahatma went alone again, swinging his lantern, and apparently at peace with himself and the whole universe.

Thereafter, King and I walked arm-in-arm, thinking in that way to lessen the risk of further pitfalls. But there was no more. The Mahatma reached at last what looked like a blind stone wall at the end of the tunnel; but there was a flagstone missing from the floor in front of it, and he disappeared down a black-dark flight of steps.

We followed him into a cellar, whose walls wept moisture, but we saw no cobras; and then up another flight of steps on the far side into a chamber that I thought I recognized. He disappeared through a door in the corner of that, and by the time we had groped our way after him he was sitting in the old black panther's cage with the brute's head in his lap, stroking and twisting its ears as if it were a kitten. The cage door was wide open, and the day was already growing hot and brassy in the east.

King and I hurried out of the cage, for the panther showed his fangs at us; the Mahatma followed us out and snapped the door shut. Instantly the panther sprang at us, trying to bend the bars together. Failing in that, he lay close and shoved his whole shoulder through, clawing at us. It was hardly any wonder that that secret, yet so simply discoverable door between Yasmini's palace and the temple-caverns was unknown.

We swung along through the great bronze gate and into the courtyard where the shrubs all stood reflected along with the marble stairway in a square pool. We plunged right in without as much as hesitating on the brink, dragging the Mahatma with us — not that he made the least objection. He laughed, and seemed to regard it as thoroughly good fun.

We splashed and fooled for a few minutes, standing neck-deep and kicking at an occasional fish as it darted by, stirring up mud with our toes until the water was so cloudy that we could see the fish no longer. Then King thought of clothes. He stood on tiptoe and shouted.

"Ismail! O — Ismail!"

Ismail came, like a yellow-fanged wolf, bowed to the Mahatma as if nakedness and royalty were one, and stood eyeing the water curiously.

"Get us garments!" King ordered testily.

"I was not staring at thee, little King *sahib*," he answered. "I was marveling!"

But he went off without explaining what he had been marveling at, and we went on with our ablutions, the job of getting ashes out of your hair not being quite so easy as it might appear. I daresay it was fifteen minutes before Ismail came back carrying two complete native costumes for King and me, and a long saffron robe for the Mahatma. Then we came out of the water and the Gray Mahatma smiled.

"I said there were no more traps, and it seems I spoke the truth," he said wonderingly. "Moreover, I did not set this trap, but it was you yourselves who led me into it."

"Which trap?" we demanded with one voice.

"You have stirred the mud, my friends, to a condition in which the *mugger* who lives in that pool is not visible. But the *mugger* is there, and I don't know why he did not seize one of you!"

In the center of the pool there was a rockery, for the benefit of plant-roots and breeding fish. I walked around it to look, and there, sure enough, lay a brute about twenty feet long, snoozing with his chin on a corner of the rock. I picked up a pole to prod him and he snapped and broke it, coming close to the edge to clatter his jaws at me. Prodding him a last time, I turned round to look for the Mahatma. He had vanished — gone as utterly and silently as a myth. King had not seen him go. We inquired of Ismail. He laughed.

"There is only one place to go — here," he answered.

"To the Princess?"

"There is nowhere else! Who shall disobey her? I have orders to unloose the panther if the *sahibs* take any other way than straight into her presence!"

CHAPTER VIII

THE RIVER OF DEATH

Dressed now in the Punjabi costume with gorgeous silk turbans, we walked side by side up the marble steps and knocked on the brass-bound, teak front door at the top. Exactly as when we arrived on the previous day, the door was immediately opened by two women.

The Mahatma was in there ahead of us, and had evidently told Yasmini sufficient of our adventures to make her laugh. She squealed with delight at sight of us.

"Come! Sit beside me in the window, both of you! My women will bring food. Afterward you shall sleep — poor things, you look as if you need it! O, what is that, Ganesha-ji? Blood on your linen? Were you hurt?"

Her swift, restless fingers drew the cloth aside and showed a few inches of where my bare skin should have been.

"It is nothing. My women shall dress it. They have oils that will cause the skin to grow again within a week. A week is nothing; you and Athelstan will be here longer than a week! And you crossed the Pool of Terrors? I have crossed that too! we three are initiates now!"

"Ye are three who will die unless discretion is the very law ye live by!" said the Gray Mahatma. He seemed annoyed about something.

"Old Dust-and-ashes!" laughed Yasmini, snapping her fingers at him. "Hah!" She laughed delightedly. "They have seen enough to make them believe what I shall tell them!"

"Woman, you woo your own destruction. None has ever set out to betray that secret and survived the first offense!" he answered.

"It was *you* who betrayed it to *me*," she said, with another golden laugh. Then, turning to King again:

"I have sought for that secret day and night! India has always known of its existence; and in every generation some have fought their way in through the outer mysteries to the knowledge within. But those who enter always become initiates, and keep the secret. I was puzzled how to begin, until I heard how, in England, a woman once overheard the secrets of Freemasonry, and was made a Freemason in consequence.

"Now behold this man they call the Gray Mahatma! He does as I tell him! You must know that these Knowers of Royal Knowledge, as they call themselves, are not the little birds in one nest that they would like to be; they quarrel among themselves, and there is a rival faction that knows only street-corner magic, but is more deadly bent on knowing Royal Knowledge than a wolf is determined to get lamb."

The Gray Mahatma saw fit to challenge some of that statement.

"It is true, that there are wolves who seek to break in," he said quietly, "but it is false that there are quarrels among ourselves."

"Hah!" That little laugh of hers was like the exclamation of a fellow who has got home with his rapier point.

"Quarrels or not," she answered, "there is a faction that was more than willing to use the ancient passage under my palace grounds, and to hold secret meetings in a room that I made ready for them."

"Faction!" The Gray Mahatma sneered. "Faithful seniors determined to expel unfaithful upstarts are not a faction!"

"At any rate," she chuckled, "they wished to hold a meeting unbeknown to the others, and they wished to make wonderful preparations for not being overheard. And I helped them — is that not so, Mahatma-ji? You see, they were scornful of women — then."

"Peace, woman!" the Mahatma growled. "Does a bee sting while it gathers honey? You spied on our secrets, but did we harm you for it?"

"You did not dare!" she retorted. "If I had been alone, you would have destroyed me along with those unfortunates on whose account you held the meeting. It would have been easy to throw me to the *mugger*. But you did not know how many women had overheard your secrets! You only knew, that more than one had, and that at least ten women witnessed the fate of your victims. Is that not so?"

"Victims is the wrong word. Call them culprits!" said the Gray Mahatma.

"What would the Government call them?" she retorted.

The Gray Mahatma curled his lip, but made no answer to that. Yasmini turned to King.

"So I knew enough of their secrets to oblige them either to kill me or else teach me all. And they did not dare kill me, because they could not kill all my women too, for fear of Government. So first they took me through that ordeal that you went through last night. And ever since then I have been trying to learn; but this science of theirs is difficult, and I suspect them of increasing the difficulty for my benefit. Nevertheless, I have mastered some of it."

"You have mastered none of it!" the Gray Mahatma retorted discourteously. "The golden light is the first step. Show me some."

"They thought they were being too clever for me," she went on. "They listened to my suggestion that it might be wise to show Athelstan King the mysteries, and send him to America to prepare the way for what is coming. So we set a trap for Athelstan. And Athelstan brought Ganesha with him. So now I have two men who know the secret, in addition to myself and all my women. And I have one man who has skill enough to *learn* the secret, now that he knows *of* it. Perhaps both men can learn it, and I know full well that one can."

"And then?" King suggested.

"You shall conquer the world!" she answered.

King smiled and said nothing.

"I am uncertain yet whether or not I shall choose to be queen of the earth!" she said. "Sometimes I think it would be fun for you and me to be absolute king and queen of everywhere. Sometimes I think it will be better to make some stupid person — say Ganesha here, for instance — king, and for ourselves to be the power behind the throne. What do *you* think, Athelstan?"

"I think," he answered.

"And you observe that the Gray Mahatma likewise thinks!" said she. "He thinks what he can do to thwart us! But I am not afraid! Oh dear no, Mahatma-ji, I am not at all fearful! Your secret is not worth ten seconds' purchase unless it is of use to me!"

"Woman, is your word worth nothing?" asked the Gray Mahatma. "You can not use what you know and keep the secret too. Let those two men escape, and the secret will be blown to the winds within the hour."

She laughed outright at him.

"They shall not escape, old raven-in-a-robe!"

Just then some of her women brought a table in, and spread it with fruit-laden dishes at the far end of the room. Yasmini rose to see whether all was as she wished it, and I got a chance, not only to look through the curtains, but also to whisper to King. He shook his head in reply to my question.

"Could you manage for two, do you think?" he asked; and by that I knew him for a vastly more than usually brave man. Consenting to what you know is sure to destroy you, if the other fellow fails, calls for courage.

"Makes a two to one chance of it," I answered.

"Very well, it's a bet. Give your orders!" said King.

The Mahatma sat rigid in mid-room with closed eyes, as if praying. His hands were crossed on his breast, and his legs twisted into a nearly unimaginable knot. He looked almost comatose.

The shutters and the glass windows were open wide to admit the morning breeze. Nothing was between us and freedom but the fluttering silk curtains and a drop of about seventy feet into an unknown river.

"Hold my hand," I said, "and jump your limit outward!"

The Gray Mahatma opened one eye and divined our intention.

"Mad!" he exclaimed. "So then that is the end of them!"

He believed what he said, for he sat still. But Yasmini came running, screaming to her women to prevent us.

King and I took off together, hand-in-hand, and I take my Bible oath that I looked up, and saw Yasmini and the Gray Mahatma leaning out of the window to watch us drown!

Of course, seventy feet is nothing much — provided you are used to the take-off, and know the water, and have a boat waiting handy to pick you up. But we had none of these advantages, and in addition to that we had the grievous handicap that King could not swim a stroke.

We took the water feet-first, close together, and that very instant I knew what we were up against. As we plunged under, we were whirled against a sunken pole that whipped and swayed in the current. King was wrenched away from me. When I fought my way to the surface I was already a hundred yards beyond the palace wall, and there was no sign of King, although I could see his turban pursuing mine down-stream. We were caught in the strongest current I had ever striven with.

I don't know what persuaded me to turn and try to swim against it for a moment. Instinct, I suppose. It was utterly impossible; I was swept along backward almost as fast as I had been traveling before. But what the effort did do was to bring me face-upstream, and so I caught sight of King clinging to a pole and being bobbed under every time the weight of water caused the pole to duck. I managed to cling to a pole myself, although like King it ducked me repeatedly, and it was perfectly evident that neither of us would be alive in the next ten minutes unless a boat should come or I should produce enough brawn and brain for two of us. And there was no boat in sight.

So between ducks I yelled to King to let go and drift down toward me. He did it; and that, I believe, is the utmost test of cold courage to which I have ever seen any man subjected; for even a strong swimmer becomes panic-stricken when he learns he is no longer master of his element. King had the self-control and pluck to lie still and drift down on me like a corpse, and I let go the pole in the nick of time to seize him as his head went under.

Followed a battle royal. Fight how I might, I could not keep both of our heads out of the water more than half the time, and King very soon lost the little breath that was left in him. Thereafter, he struggled a bit, but that did not last long, and presently he became unconscious. I believed he was dead.

The choice then seemed to lie between drowning too or letting go of him. I did not dare try the shallows, for ninety per cent. of them are quicksands in that river, and more than one army has perished in the effort to force its way across. The only possible safety lay in keeping to mid-stream and sweeping along with the current until something should turn up — a boat — a log — possibly a backwater, or even the breakwater of a bridge.

So I decided to drown, and to annoy the angels of the underworld by taking as long as possible in the process. And I set to work to fight as I had never in my whole life fought before. It was like swimming in a millrace. The current swirled us this and that way, but everlastingly forward.

Sometimes the current rolled us over and over on each other, but for fifty per cent. of the time I managed to keep King on top of me, I swimming on my back and holding him by both arms, head nearly out of the water. I can't explain exactly why I went to all that trouble, for I was convinced he was dead.

I remember wondering what the next world was going to be like, and whether King and I would meet there, or whether we would each be sent to a sphere suited to our individual requirements — and if so, what my sphere would be like, and whether either of us would ever meet Yasmini, and what she would be doing there. But it never occurred to me once that Athelstan King might be alive yet, or that he and I would be presently treading mother earth again.

I remember several terrific minutes when a big tree came whirling toward us in an eddy, and my legs got tangled up in some part of it that was under water. Then, when I managed to struggle free, King's cotton loin-cloth became wrapped in a tangle of twigs and I could neither wrench nor break him free; whenever I tried it I merely sent myself under and pulled his head after me.

However, that tree suggested the possibility of prolonging the agony a while.

I seized a branch and tried to take advantage of it, using all my strength and skill to keep the tree from rolling over on King and submerging him completely. I can remember when we whirled under the steel bridge and the tree struck the breakwater of the middle pier; that checked us for a moment, and instead of sending us under, dragged King half out of the water, so that he lay after that on top of a branch.

Then the stream got us going again, and swung the butt end of the tree around so that I was forced by it backward through the arch of the bridge; and after that for more than a mile we were waltzed round and round past sand-banks where the alligators lay on the look-out for half-burned corpses from the burning ghats higher up.

At last we swung round a curve in the river and came on a quiet bay where they were washing elephants. The current swung the tree inshore to a point where it struck a submerged sand-bank and stuck there; and there we lay with the current racing by, and King bobbing up and down with his head out of water, and I too weak by that time to break off the twig around which his loin-cloth was wrapped.

Well, there we were; but after a few minutes I raised enough steam for the whistle at all events. I yelled until my own ear-drums seemed to be bursting and my lungs ached from the pressure on the water in them, and after what seemed an eternity one of the mahouts on shore heard me.

Hope surged triumphant! I could see him wave his arm, and already I saw visions of dry land again, and a disappointed Yama! But I was overlooking one important point: we were in India, where rescues are not undertaken in a hurry.

He called a conference. I saw all the mahouts gather together in one place and stare at us and talk. They swung their arms as they argued. I don't know what argument it was that finally appealed to the mahouts, but after an interminable session one of them fetched a long rope and nine or ten of them climbed on the backs of three big elephants. They worked their way a little bit upstream, and then came as close as the elephants dared. One of the big brutes felt his way cautiously to within twenty yards, and then threw up his trunk and refused to budge another inch.

At that a lean, naked, black man stood up on his rump and paid out the rope down-stream. He had to make nine or ten attempts before it finally floated within reach of my hand. Then I made it fast to the tree and, taking King in my right arm, started to work my way along it. It was just as well I did that, and got clear of the branch; for the mahouts passed the rope around the elephant's neck and set him to hauling; he rolled the tree over and over, and that would surely have been the end of King and me if we had been within reach of the overturning branches. As it was I clung to the rope and the elephant hauled the lot of us high and dry.

CHAPTER IX

THE EARTHQUAKE ELEPHANT

At the end of a minute's examination I began to suspect that King was not quite dead, so I recalled the old life-saver's drill and got to work on him. It took time. As King came more and more to his senses, and vomited a bit, and began to behave in all ways like a living man again, I had a chance to talk to the mahouts; and they were just like the members of any other union, preferring conversation to alleged hard labor any day of the week. They told me why the elephants were being washed so early and we enjoyed a regular *conversazione* on the beach.

It appeared the elephants were wanted to take part in a procession, and for a while they let me guess what sort of a procession. But at last they took compassion on my ignorance.

"*She* has issued invitations to a party for princesses in *her panch mahal*!"

Who was *she*? Everybody knew who *she* was!

"The Princess Yasmini?" I suggested.

Whereat they all chuckled and made grimaces, and did everything except acknowledge her name in public.

And then suddenly Athelstan King decided to sit up and spat some more water out and tried to laugh. And they thought that was so exquisitely funny that they all laughed too.

Then, when he had coughed a little more —

"We're going to attend that party!"

"Why?" I asked him.

"Two reasons." But he had to cough up more water before he could tell them. "One: The Gray Mahatma will never rest until he knows we're dead, or done for, and the safest place is close to the enemy; and, two: I never will rest until I know the secret of that science of theirs!"

"How in thunder are we going to get back?" I objected.

"Ride!" he suggested.

"How — when — where?"

"Elephant — now — to her palace," he answered.

"They're not her elephants."

"So much the better! She'll think the Maharajah knows all about us. She'll *have* to accord us protection after that."

He asked a dozen more questions, and finally struggled to his feet.

"My friend," he said then to the chief mahout, "if you propose to take us two *sahibs* to *her* palace, and be back at your master's stables in time to get ready for the *Bibi-kana*, you'll have to hurry!"

"But I did not propose it!" the mahout answered.

"Nay, the gods proposed it. Which is your fastest elephant?"

"That great one yonder — Akbar. But who is giving orders? We are a maharajah's servants."

"The gods are ordering all this business!" King assured him. "I wish to ride to *her* palace."

"By *her* leave?"

"By the gods' leave."

"Will the gods pay me?"

"Doubtless. But she will pay first — setting the gods a good example."

The native of India finds it perfectly convenient to ride on a six-inch plank, slung more or less like a house-painter's platform against an elephant's bulging ribs, and it does not seem to make much difference to him when more weight is on one side than on the other. But King and I had to stand and hold each other's hands across the pad; and even so we were by no means too secure, for Akbar resented being taken away from the herd and behaved like a mutinous earthquake.

It was not so far to the city by road, because the river wound a good deal and the road cut straight from point to point. But it was several miles, and we covered it at pretty nearly the speed of a railroad train.

In spite of his rage, Akbar had perfect control of himself. Having missed about half his morning swim, and the herd's society, he proposed to miss nothing else, and there was not one cart, one *ekka*, one piled-up load in all those miles that he did not hit and do his utmost to destroy. There was not one yellow dog that he did not give chase to and try to trample on.

He stopped to pull the thatch from the roof of a little house beside the road, but as the plying *ankus* made his head ache he couldn't stay long enough to finish that job but scooted uproad again in full pursuit of a Ford car, while an angry man shoved his head through the hole in the roof of the house and cursed all the rumps of all the elephants, together with the forebears and descendants of their owners and their wives.

It seemed that Akbar was fairly well-known thereabouts. The men in the Ford car shouted the news in advance of his coming, and the road into the city began to look like the track of a routed army. Every man and animal took to his heels, and Akbar trumpeted wild hurrahs as he strained all tendons in pursuit. He needed no second wind, because he never lost his first, but he took the whole course as far as the city gate at a speed that would have satisfied Jehu, son of Nimshi, who, the Bible says, made Israel to sin.

That particular city gate consisted of an arch, covered with carvings of outrageous-looking gods, and as a picture display it was perfect, but as an entrance to a crowded city it possessed no virtue. It was so narrow that only one vehicle could pass at a time, and the whole swarm jammed between it and us like sticks in front of a drain.

And not even Akbar's strength was so great that he could shove them through, so the ancient problem of an irresistible force in contact with an immovable object was presented, and solved by Akbar after a fashion of his own.

He picked the softest spot, which was a wain-load of cotton bales, and upset it, cannoning off that cushion so swiftly as to come within an ace of scattering his four passengers across the landscape; and discerning, with a swift strategic eye that would have done credit to the dashingest cavalry general, that that rout was complete and nothing could be gained by adding to it, he headed for the river and the women's bathing place, took the broad stone steps at a dead run, and plunged straight in.

No ship was ever launched with more perfect aplomb, nor floated more superbly on an even keel than did Akbar at the women's bathing ghat. For a moment I thought he proposed to lie down there and finish his interrupted toilet, but he contented himself with squirting water on the sore spot caused by the thumping *ankus* of the driver's and set out to swim upstream.

It was not until he had reached the second ghat and climbed the steps there that Akbar put himself in Napoleon's class. When he reached the top of the steps no amount of whacking with the *ankus* could make him turn to the right and follow the city street. He turned to the left, tooted a couple of wild hurrahs through his newly wetted whistle, and raced to meet the traffic as it struggled through the gate in single file!

There was ruin ripe for harvest and it looked like the proper time to jump. But suddenly — with that delightful wheeled panic at his mercy, the big brute stopped, stood still and looked at them, muttering and gurgling to himself. Instantly the mahout began petting him, calling him endearing names and praising his wisdom and discretion. I can't swear that the beast understood what was said to him, but he acted exactly as if he did. He picked up dust from the street with his trunk, blew a little of it in the general direction of the defeated enemy, blew a little more on himself, and turned his rump toward the gate, as if to signify that hostilities were over!

As he did that, a man who was something of an athlete swung himself up on the off-side footboard, and a second later the proud face of the Gray Mahatma confronted me across the saddle-pad alongside King's!

"You are heavy enough to balance the two of us," he said, as if no other comment were necessary. "Why did you run away from me? You can never escape!"

Well, of course anybody could say that after he had found us again.

"Was it you who checked this elephant?" I asked him, remembering what he had done to the black panther and the snakes, but he did not answer.

"Where do you think you are going?" I asked.

"That is what the dry leaves asked of the wind," he answered. "An observant eye is better than a yearning ear, and patience outwears curiosity!"

Suddenly I recalled a remark that King had made on the beach and it dawned on me that by frightening the mahout into silence the Mahatma might undo the one gain we had made by that plunge and swim. As long as the Maharajah who owned the elephant was to hear about our adventure, all was well. News of us would reach the Government. Most of the maharajahs are pro-British, because their very existence as reigning princes depends on that attitude, and they can be relied on to report to the British authorities any irregularity whatever that comes under their notice and at the same time does not incriminate themselves.

The same thought probably occurred to King, but he was rather too recently recovered from drowning to be quick yet off the mark and besides, the Mahatma was between him and the mahout, whereas I had a free field. So I tugged at the arm of the second mahout, who was sitting behind his chief, and he scrambled down beside me.

The Mahatma tried to take immediate advantage of that, and the very thing he did made it all the easier for me to deal with the second mahout, who had made the trip with us and who stared into my face with a kind of puzzled mistrust. The Mahatma, as active as a cat, climbed up behind the chief mahout and sat astride the elephant's neck in the place where the second mahout had been, and began whispering.

"What is your Maharajah's name?" I asked my neighbor on the plank.

"Jihanbihar," he answered, giving a string of titles too that had no particular bearing on the situation. They sounded like a page of the Old Testament.

"You observe that his favorite elephant is about to be stolen with the aid of the Gray Mahatma!"

The fellow nodded, and the expression of his face was not exactly pleased; he may have been one of a crowd that got cursed by the Mahatma for asking too many impertinent questions.

"He has a reputation, that Mahatma, hasn't he?" I suggested. "You have heard of the miracles that he performs?"

He nodded again.

"You see that he is talking to the chief mahout now? Take my word for it, he is casting a spell on him! Would you like to have him cast a spell on you too?"

He shook his head.

"Run swiftly then, and tell the Maharajah *sahib* to get a Brahman to cancel the spell, and you will be rewarded. Go quickly."

He dropped from the plank and went off at a run just as the Mahatma turned and saw him. The Mahatma had been whispering in the mahout's ear, and as his eye met mine I laughed. For a moment he watched the man running, and then, as if to demonstrate what a strange mixture of a man he was, he laughed back at me. He acknowledged defeat instantly, and did not appear in the least annoyed by it, but on the contrary appeared to accord me credit for outwitting him, as undoubtedly I had.

India is not a democratic country. Nobody is troubled about keeping the underworld in its place, so mahout or sweeper has the ear of majesty as readily as any other man, if not even more so. And it would not make the slightest difference now what kind of cock and bull story the mahout might tell to the Maharajah. However wild it might be it would certainly include the fact that two white men had ridden to Yasmini's palace on the Maharajah's favorite elephant after having been fished out of the river by mahouts at the elephant's bathing ghat.

It was the likeliest thing in the world that representations would be made that very afternoon by telegraph to the nearest important British official, who would feel compelled to make inquiries. The British Government can not afford to have even unknown white men mysteriously made away with.

The Gray Mahatma took all that for granted and nodded comprehendingly. His smile, as we neared Yasmini's palace gate, appeared to me to include a perfect appreciation of the situation. He seemed to accept it as candidly as he had acknowledged my frequent escapes the night before.

Ismail opened the gate without demur and Akbar sauntered in, being used to palaces. He passed under the first arch into the second courtyard, coming to a halt at a gate on the far side that was too small for his enormous bulk where he proceeded to kneel without waiting for instructions.

"Do you feel proud?" the Mahatma asked me unexpectedly as he climbed off Akbar's neck.

Suspecting some sort of verbal trap I did not answer him.

"You are like this elephant. You are able to do irreparable damage if you see fit. *She* was as apt as usual when she dubbed you Ganesha!"

He was working toward some point he intended to make, like one of those pleasant-tongued attorneys flattering a witness before tying him up in a knot, so I was careful to say nothing whatever. King came around the kneeling elephant and joined us, leaning back against the beast and appraising the Mahatma with his eyes half-closed.

"You're dealing with white men," King suggested. "Why don't you talk in terms that we understand?"

It seemed difficult for the Mahatma to descend to that. He half-closed his eyes in turn and frowned, as if hard put to it to simplify his thoughts sufficiently — something like a mathematician trying to explain himself to the kindergarten class.

"I could kill you," he said, looking straight at King.

King nodded.

"You are not the kind of man who *should* be killed," he went on.

"Did you ever hear the fable of the fox and the sour grapes?" King asked him, and the Mahatma looked annoyed.

"Would you rather be killed?" he retorted.

"'Pon my soul, I'm inclined to leave that to the outcome," King answered. "Death would mean investigation, and investigation discovery of that science you gave us a glimpse of."

"If I was to let you go," the Mahatma began to argue.

"I would not go! Forward is the only way," King interrupted. "You've a reason for not having us two men killed. What is it?"

"I have no reason whatever for preserving this one's life," the Mahatma answered, glancing at me casually. "For reasons beyond my power of guessing he seems to bear a charmed existence, but he has my leave to visit the next world, and his departure would by no means inconvenience me. But you are another matter."

"How so?" King asked. "Mr. Ramsden is the man who would be inquired for. The Indian Government, whose servant I no longer am, might ignore me, but the multi-millionaire who is Mr. Ramsden's partner would spend millions and make an international scandal."

"I am thinking of you, not of him. I am thinking you are honest," said the Gray Mahatma, looking into King's eyes.

"So is he," King answered.

"I am wondering whether or not you are honest enough to trust me," said the Gray Mahatma.

"Why certainly!" King answered. "If you would commit yourself I would trust you. Why not?"

"But this man would not," said the Mahatma, nudging me as if I were the elephant.

"I trust my friend King," I retorted. "If he decides to trust you, I stand back of him."

"Very well then, let us exchange promises."

"Suppose we go a little more cautiously and discuss them first," suggested King.

"I will promise both of you your life, your eventual freedom, and my friendship. Will you promise me not to go in league with *her* —"

"I'll agree to that unconditionally!" King assured him with a dry smile.

" — not to try to learn the secret of the science — — "

"Why not?"

"Because if you *should* try I could never save your lives."

"Well, what else?"

"Will you take oath never to disclose the whereabouts of the entrance to the caverns in which you were allowed to see the sciences?"

"I shall have to think that over."

"Furthermore, will you promise to take whatever means is pointed out to you of helping India to independence?"

"What do you mean by independence?"

"Self-government."

"I've been working for that ever since I cut my eye-teeth," answered King. "So has every other British officer and civil servant who has any sense of public duty."

"Will you continue to work for it, and employ the means that shall be pointed out to you?"

"Yes is the answer to the first part. Can't answer the second part until I've studied the means."

"Will you join me in preventing that princess from throwing the world into fresh confusion?"

"Dunno about joining you. It's part of my business to prevent her little game," King answered.

"She has proven herself almost too clever, even for us," said the Mahatma. "She spied on us, and she hid so many witnesses behind a wall pierced with holes that it would be impossible for us to make sure of destroying all of them. And somewhere or other she has hidden an account of what she knows, so that if anything should happen to her it would fall into the hands of the Government and compel investigation."

"Wise woman!" King said smiling.

"Yes! But not so altogether wise. Hitherto we fooled her for all her cleverness. Her price of silence was education in our mysteries, and we have made the education incomprehensible."

"Then why do you want my help?"

"Because she has a plan now that is so magnificent in its audacity as to baffle even our secret council!"

King whistled, and the Mahatma looked annoyed — whether with himself or King I was not sure.

"That is what I have been hunting for three years — your secret council. I knew it existed; never could prove it," said King.

"Can you prove it now?" asked the Mahatma with even more visible annoyance.

"I think so. You'll have to help me."

"I?"

"You or the Princess!" King answered. "Shall I join you or her?"

"Thou fool! There was a sheep who asked, 'Which shall I run with, tiger or wolf?' Consider that a moment!"

King showed him the courtesy of considering it, and was silent for perhaps two minutes, during which the mahout judged it opportune to whine forth his own demands. But nobody took any notice of him.

"You seem check-mate to me," King said at last. "You daren't kill my friend or me. You daren't make away with us. You daren't make away with the Princess. The Princess and several of her women know enough of your secret to be able to force your hand; so do my friend Mr. Ramsden and I. Mr. Ramsden and I have seen sufficient in that madhouse underneath the temple to compel a Government inquiry. Is it peace or war, Mahatma? Will you introduce me to your secret council, or will you fight to a finish?"

"I would rather not fight with you, my young friend."

"Introduce me, then," King answered, smiling.

"You don't know what you ask — what that involves."

"But I propose to know," said King.

The Mahatma never seemed to mind acknowledging defeat.

"I see you are determined," he said quietly. "Determination, my young friend, combined with ignorance, is a murderer nine times out of ten. However, you do not understand that, and you are determined, I have no authority to make such terms as you propose, but I will submit the matter to those whom you desire to meet. Does that satisfy you?"

King looked immensely dissatisfied.

"I would rather be your friend than your enemy," he answered.

"So said light and darkness each to the other when they first met! You shall have your answer presently. In the mean time will you try not to make my task even more difficult than it already is?"

King laughed uncomfortably.

"Mahatma, I like you well enough, but no terms until I have your answer! Sorry! I'd like to be friends with you."

"The pity of it is that though you are honestly determined you are bound to fail," the Mahatma answered; and at that he dismissed the whole subject with a motion of one hand, and turned toward Ismail, who was lurking about in the shadows like a wolf.

The Mahatma sent the man to the door of the *panch mahal* with a message that money was needed; and the mahout spent the next ten minutes in loud praises of his kneeling elephant, presumably on the theory that "it pays to advertise," for it is not only the West that worships at that shrine.

When Ismail came back with a tray on which were several little heaps of money the mahout went into abject ecstasies of mingled jubilee and reverence. His mouth betrayed unbelief and his eyes glinted avarice. His fingers twitched with agonied anticipation, and he began to praise his elephant again, as some people recite proverbs to keep themselves from getting too excited.

The various heaps of money on the tray must have amounted to about fifty dollars. The mahout spread out the end of his turban by way of begging bowl, and the Mahatma shook all the money into it, so that Ismail gasped and the mahout himself turned up his eyes in exquisite delirium.

"Go or you will be too late!" was all the Mahatma said to him, and the mahout did not wait for a second command, but mounted his elephant's neck, kicked the big brute up and rode away, in a hurry to be off before he should wake up and discover that the whole adventure was a dream.

But he could not get away with it as easily as all that. Ismail was keeper of the gate, and the gate was locked. Akbar doubtless could have broken down the gate if so instructed, but even the East, which is never long on gratitude, would hardly do that much damage after receiving such a royal largesse. Ismail went to unlock the gate, and demanded his percentage, giving it, though, the Eastern name, which means "the usual thing."

And the usual argument took place — I approached to listen to it — the usual recriminations, threats, counterclaims, abuse, appeals to various deaf deities, and finally concession — after Ismail had made the all-compelling threat to tell the other mahouts how much the gift had amounted to. I suppose it was instinct that suggested that idea. At any rate, it worked and the mahout threw a handful of coins to him.

Thereat, of course, there was immediate, immense politeness on both sides. Ismail prayed that Allah might make the mahout as potbellied and idle as his elephant; and the mahout suggested to a dozen corruptible deities that Ismail might be happier with a thousand children and wives who were true to him. Whereat Ismail opened the gate, and Akbar helped himself liberally to sugar-cane from a passing wagon; so that every one was satisfied except the rightful owner of the sugar-cane, who cursed and wept and called Akbar an honest rajah, by way I suppose of expressing his opinion of all the tax-levying powers that be.

There happened to be a thing they call a "constabeel" going by, and the owner of the sugar-cane appealed to him for justice and relief. So the "constabeel" prodded Akbar's rump with his truncheon, and helped himself, too, to sugar-cane by way of balancing accounts. And while the owner of the sugar-cane was bellowing red doctrine about that, Ismail went out and helped himself likewise, only more liberally, carrying in an armful of the stuff, and slamming the gate in the faces of all concerned. In cynical enjoyment of the blasphemy outside he sat down then in the shadow of the wall to chew the cane and count the change extorted from the mahout.

"Behold India self-governed!" I said, turning to beckon through the arch between the two courtyards.

But the Mahatma was gone! And unlike the Cheshire cat, he had not even left a smile behind him — had not even left Athelstan King behind him. The two had disappeared as silently and as utterly as if they had never been there!

CHAPTER X

A DATE WITH DOOM

I hunted about, looked around corners, searched the next court-yard, and drew blank. Then I asked Ismail, and he mocked me.

"The Mahatma? You are like those fools who pursue virtue. There never was any!"

"That mahout named you rightly just now," said I. "He knew your character perfectly."

"That may be," Ismail answered, rising to his feet. "But he was on an elephant where I could not reach him. You think you are a strong man? Feel of that then!"

He was old, but no mean adversary. Luckily for him he did not draw a knife. I hugged the wind out of him, whirled him until he was dizzy and threw him down into his dog's corner by the gate, not much the worse except for a bruise or two.

"Now!" I said. "Which way went King sahib and the Gray Mahatma?"

"All ways are one, and the one way leads to *her!*"

That was all I could get out of him. So I took the one way, straight down through the courtyards and under the arches, past the old black panther's cage — the way that King and I had taken when we first arrived. But it seemed like a year since I had trodden those ancient flagstones side by side with King — more than a year! It seemed as if a dozen lifetimes intervened. And it also occurred to me that I was growing famished and desperately sleepy, and I knew that King must be in even worse condition. The old, black panther was sleeping as I went by, and I envied him.

There was a choice of two ways when I reached the *panch mahal*, for it was feasible to enter through the lower door, which was apparently unguarded, and climb the stone stairway that wound inside the wall. However, I chose the marble front steps, and barked my knuckles on the door at the top.

I was kept waiting several minutes, and then four women opened it in place of the customary two; and instead of smiling, as on previous occasions, they frowned, lining up across the threshold. They were older women than the others had been and looked perfectly capable of showing fight; allowing for their long pins and possible hidden weapons I would not have given ten cents for my chance against them. So I asked for King and the Mahatma.

They pretended not to understand. They knew no Hindustani. My dialect of Punjabi was as Greek to them. They knew nothing about my clothes, or the suitcase that King and I shared between us and that, according to Yasmini, had been carried by her orders to the palace. The words "King" and "Mahatma" seemed to convey no meaning to them. They made it perfectly obvious that they suspected me of being mad.

I began to suspect myself of the same thing! Feeling as sleepy as I did, it was not unreasonable to suspect myself at any rate of dreaming; yet I had sufficient power of reasoning left to argue that if those were dream-women they would give way in front of me. So I stepped straight forward, and they no more gave way than a she-bear will if you call on her when she is nursing cubs. Two more women stepped out from behind the curtains with long slithery daggers in their hands, and somehow I was not minded to test whether those were dream-daggers or not.

It was a puzzle to know what to do. The one unthinkable thing would be to leave King unsought for. Suddenly it occurred to me to try that door underneath the steps; so I kissed my hand irreverently to the quarterguard of harridans, and turned my back on them — which I daresay was the most unwise move that I ever made in my whole life. I have done things that were more disastrous in the outcome, but never anything more deserving of ruin.

Have you ever been tackled, tripped and hog-tied by women? Run rather than risk it!

They threw a rope over my shoulders from behind, and I felt the foot of one termagant in the small of my back as she hauled taut. I spun round and stepped forward to slacken the noose and free myself, and two more nooses went over my head in swift succession. Another caught my right foot — another my right hand! More women came, with more ropes. It was only a matter of seconds before they were almost dragging me asunder as they hauled, two hags to a rope, and every one of them straining as if the game were tug-of-war.

There was nothing else to do, and plenty of inducement, so I did it. I yelled. I sent my voice bellowing through those echoing halls to such tune that if King were anywhere in the place he would have to hear me. But it did me no good. They only produced a gag and added that to my discomfort, shoving a great lump of rubber in my mouth and wrapping a towel over it so tightly that I could hardly breathe.

Then came Yasmini, gorgeously amused, standing at the top of the steps where the inner hall was raised a few feet above the outer, and ordering me blindfolded as well as rendered dumb.

"For if he can see as well as he can roar he will presently know too much," she explained sarcastically.

So they wrapped another towel over my eyes and pinned it with a cursed export safety-pin that pierced clean through my scalp. And the harder I struggled, the tighter they pulled on the ropes and the louder Yasmini laughed, until I might as well have been on that rack that King and I saw in the cavern underneath the temple.

"So strong *Ganesha-ji!*" she mocked. "So strong and yet so impotent! Such muscles! Look at them! Can the buffalo hear, or are his ears stopped too?"

A woman rearranged the head-towel to make sure that my ears were missing nothing; after which Yasmini purred her pleasantest.

"O buffalo Ganesha, I would have you whipped to death if I thought that would not anger Athelstan! What do you mistake me for? Me, who have been twice a queen! That was a mighty jump from my window; and even as the buffalo you swam, Ganesha! Buffalo, buffalo! Who but a buffalo would snatch my Athelstan away from me, and then return alone! What have you done with him? Hah! You would like to answer that you have done nothing with him — buffalo, buffalo! He would never have left you willingly, nor you him — you two companions who share one foolish little bag between you!

"Does he love you? Hope, Ganesha! Hope that he loves you! For unless he comes to find you, Ganesha, all the horrors that you saw last night, and all the deaths, and all the tortures shall be yours — with alligators at last to abolish the last traces of you! Do you like snakes, Ganesha? Do you like a madhouse in the dark? I think not. Therefore, Ganesha, you shall be left to yourself to think a little while. Think keenly! Invent a means of finding Athelstan and I will let you go free for his sake. But — fail — to think — of a successful plan — Ganesha — and you shall suffer in every atom of your big body! Bass! Take him away!"

I was frog-marched, and flung face-downward on to cushions, after which I heard a door snap shut and had leisure to work myself free from the ropes and gag and towels. It took time, for the hussies had drawn the cords until they bit into the muscles, and maybe I was twenty minutes about getting loose. Then, for ten minutes more I sat and chafed the rope-cuts, craving food, examining the room, and wishing above all things that conscience would let me fall asleep on the feathery, scented pillows with which the floor was strewn, rather than stay awake on the off-chance of discovering where King might be.

It was practically a bare room, having walls of painted wood that sounded solid when I made the circuit of the floor and tapped each panel in turn. But that proved nothing, for even the door sounded equally solid; the folk who built that palace used solid timber, not veneer, and as I found out afterward the door was nearly a foot thick. On the floor I could make no impression whatever by thumping, and there was no furniture except the pillows — nothing that I could use for a weapon.

But there were the cotton ropes with which they had bound me, and before doing anything else I knotted them all into one. I had no particular reason for doing that beyond the general principle that one long rope is usually better than a half-a-dozen short ones in most emergencies.

There was only one window, and that was perhaps two feet high, big enough, that is, to scramble through, but practically inaccessible, and barred. The only weapon I had was that infernal brass safety-pin that had held the towel to my scalp, and I stuck that away in my clothes like a magpie hiding things on general principles.

I began to wonder whether it would not be wisest after all to lie down and sleep. But I was too hungry to sleep, and it was recognition of that fact which produced the right idea.

Beyond doubt Yasmini realized that I was hungry. She had threatened me with tortures, and was likely to inflict them if she should think that necessary; but nothing seemed more unlikely than that she would keep me for the present without food and water. It would be bad strategy, to say the least of it. She had admitted that she did not want to offend King.

The more I considered that, the more worth while it seemed to bet on it; and as I had nothing to bet with except will power and personal convenience, I plunged with both and determined to stay awake as long as human endurance could hold out.

There was only one way that food could possibly be brought

into the room, and that was through the massive teak-wood door. It was in the middle of the wall, and opened inward; there were no bolts on the inside. Anybody opening it cautiously would be able to see instantly all down the length of half that wall, and possibly two thirds of the room as well.

It would have been hardly practical to stand against the door and hit at the first head that showed, for then if the door should open suddenly, it would strike me and give the alarm. There was nothing else for it but to stand well back against the wall on the side of the door on which the hinges were; and as that would make the range too long for quick action I had to invent some other means of dealing with the owner of the first head than jumping in and punching it.

There was nothing whatever to contrive a trap with but the cotton rope and the safety-pin, but the safety-pin like Mohammed's Allah, "made all things possible." I stuck that safety-pin in the woodwork and hung the noose in such position that the least jerk would bring it down over an intruding head — practised the stunt for ten or fifteen minutes, and then got well back against the wall with the end of the line in hand, and waited.

I have read Izaak Walton, and continue unconvinced. I still class fishing and golf together with tiddledywinks, and eschew all three as thoughtfully as I avoid bazaars and "crushes" given by the ladies of both sexes. The rest of that performance was too much like fishing with a worm to suit my temperament, and although I caught more in the end than I ever took with rod and line, the next half-hour was boredom pure and simple, multiplied to the point of torture by intense yearning for sleep.

But patience sometimes is rewarded. I very nearly was asleep when the sound of a bolt being drawn on the far side of the door brought every sense to the alert with that stinging feeling that means blood spurting through your veins after a spell of lethargy. The bolt was a long time drawing, as if some one were afraid of making too much noise, and I had plenty of time to make sure that my trap was in working order.

And when the door opened gingerly at last, a head inserted itself, my noose fell, and I hauled taut, I don't know which was most surprised — myself or the Gray Mahatma! I jerked the noose so tight that he could not breathe, let alone argue the point. I reckon I nearly hanged him, for his neck jammed against the door, and I did not dare let go for fear he might withdraw himself and collapse on the wrong side. I wanted him *in*side, and in a hurry.

He was about two-thirds unconscious when I seized him by his one long lock of hair and hauled him in, shutting the door again and leaning my weight against it, while I pried the noose free to save him from sure death. Those cotton ropes don't render the way a hemp one would. And while I was doing that a sickening, utterly unexpected sound announced that somebody outside the door had cautiously shot the bolt again! The Mahatma and I were both prisoners!

I sat the old fellow down on a cushion in a corner and chafed his neck until the blood performed its normal office of revivifying him. And as he slowly opened first one eye and then the other, instead of cursing me as I expected, he actually smiled.

"The quality of your mercy was rather too well strained," he said in English, "but I thank you for the offer nevertheless!"

"Offer?" I answered. "What offer have I made you?"

"A very friendly offer. But the penalty of being in the secret of our sciences is that we may not die, except in the service of the cause. Therefore, my friend, your goodwill fell on barren ground, for if you had succeeded in killing me my obligation would have been held to pass to you, and you would have suffered terribly."

"Who locked the door on us just now?" I asked him.

"I don't know," he answered, smiling whimsically.

"Very well," I said, "suppose you work one of your miracles! You and King disappeared a while ago simply perfectly from right alongside me. Can you repeat the process here and spirit me away?"

He shook his head.

"My friend, if your eyes had not been fixed on things unworthy of consideration such as an elephant's rump and the theft of sugar-cane, you would have seen us go."

"How did you persuade King to leave me standing there without a word of warning?" I demanded.

"How were you persuaded into this place?" he retorted.

"You mean you gagged and bound him?"

He smiled again.

"Your friend was weak from having so nearly been drowned; nevertheless, you overestimate my powers!"

"When I first met you, you gripped my hand," I answered. "I am reckoned a strong man, yet I could not shift your hand a fraction of an inch. Now you suggest that you are weaker than a half-drowned man. I don't understand you."

"Of course you don't. That is because you don't understand the form of energy that I used on the first occasion. Unfortunately I can only use it when arrangements have been made in advance. It is as mechanical as your watch, only a different kind of mechanics — something, in fact, that some of your Western scientists would say has not yet been invented."

"Well, where's King?" I asked him.

"Upstairs. He asked me to bring you. Now how can I?"

He smiled again with that peculiar whimsical helplessness that contrasted so strangely with his former arrogance. He who had looked like a lion when we first encountered him seemed now to be a meek and rather weak old man — much weaker in fact than could be accounted for by the red ring that my noose had made on his neck.

"Is King at liberty?" I demanded.

"And what do you call liberty?" he asked me blandly, as if he were really curious to know my opinion on that subject.

"Can he come and go without molestation?"

"If he cares to run that risk, and is not caught. Try not to become impatient with me! Anger is impotence! Explanations that do not explain are part and parcel of all religions and most sciences; therefore why lose your temper? Your friend is free to come and go, but must take his chance of being caught. He pursues investigations."

"Where?"

"Where else than in this palace? Listen!"

Among all the phenomena of nature there is none more difficult to explain than sound. Hitherto in that teak-lined room we had seemed shut off from the rest of the world completely, for the door and walls were so thick and the floor so solid that sound-waves seemed unable to penetrate. Yet now a noise rather like sandpaper being chafed together began to assert itself so distinctly as to seem almost to have its origin in the room. In a way it resembled the forest noise when a breeze stirs the tree-tops at night — irregular enough, and yet with a kind of pulse in it, increasing and decreasing.

"You recognize that?" asked the Mahatma.

I shook my head.

"Veiled women, walking!"

"You mean the princesses have come?"

"A few, and their attendants."

"How many princesses?"

"Oh, not more than twenty. But each will bring at the least twenty attendants, and perhaps a score of friends, each of whom in turn will have her own attendants. And only the princesses and their friends will enter the audience hall, which, however, will be surrounded by the attendants, whose business it will be to see that no stranger, and above all no male shall see or overhear."

"And if they were to catch Athelstan King up there?"

"That would be his last and least pleasant experience in this world!"

That was easy enough to believe. I had just had an experience of what those palace women could do.

"She, who learned our secrets, will take care that none shall play that trick on *her*," the Mahatma went on confidently. "These women will use the audience hall she lent to us. Their plan is to control the new movement in India, and their strength consists in secrecy. They will take all precautions."

"Do you mean to tell me," I demanded, "that as you sit here now you are impotent? Can't you work any of your tricks?"

"Those are not tricks, my friend, they are sciences. Can your Western scientists perform to order without their right environment and preparations?"

"Then you can't break that door down, or turn loose any magnetic force?"

"You speak like a superstitious fool," he retorted calmly. "The answer is no."

"That," said I, "is all that I was driving at. Do you see this?" And I held my right fist sufficiently close to his nose to call urgent attention to it. "Tell me just what transpired between you and King from the time when you disappeared out there in the court-yard until you came in here alone!"

"No beating in the world could make me say a word," he answered calmly. "You would only feel horribly ashamed."

I believed him, and sat still, he looking at me in a sort of way in which a connoisseur studies a picture with his eyelids a little lowered.

"Nevertheless," he went on presently, "I observe that I have misjudged you in some respects. You are a man of violent temper, which is cave-man foolishness; yet you have prevailing judgment, which is the beginning of civilization. There is no reason why I should not tell you what you desire to know, even though it will do you no good."

"I listen," I answered, trying to achieve that air of humility with which *chelas* listen to their *gurus*.

That was partly because I really respected the man in a way; and partly because there was small harm in flattering him a little, if that could induce him to tell me the more.

"Know then," he began, "that it was my fault that the Princess Yasmini was able to play that trick on us. It was to me that she first made the proposal that we should use her audience hall for our conference. It was I who conveyed that proposal to those whom it concerned, and I who persuaded them. It was through my lack of diligence that the hiding-place was overlooked in which she and certain of her women lay concealed, so that they overheard some of our secrets.

"For that I should have been condemned to death at once, and it would have been better if that had been done.

"Yet for fifty years I have been a man of honor. And although it is one of our chief requirements that we lay aside such foolishness as sentiment, nevertheless the seeds of sentiment remained, and those men were loath to enforce the penalty on me, who had taught so many of them.

"So they compromised, which is inevitably fatal. For compromise bears within itself the roots of right and wrong, so that whatever good may come of it must nevertheless be ruined by inherent evil. I bade them use me for their studies, and have done with compromise, but being at fault my authority was gone, so they had their way.

"They imposed on me the task of making use of the Princess Yasmini, and of employing her by some means to make a beginning of the liberation of India. And she sought to make use of me to get Athelstan King into her clutches. Moreover, believing that her influence over us was now too great to be resisted, she demanded that Athelstan King and yourself should be shown sciences; and I consented, believing that thereby your friend might be convinced, and would agree to go to the United States to shape public opinion.

"Thereafter you know what happened. You know also that, because the seeds of compromise were inherent in the plan, my purpose failed. Instead of consenting to go to the United States Athelstan King insisted on learning our sciences. You and he escaped, by a dive from the upper window of this palace that would not have disgraced two fish-hawks, and although you never guessed it, by that dive you sentenced me to death.

"For I had to report your escape to those whom it most concerned. And at once it was obvious to them that you were certain to tell what you had seen.

"Nevertheless, there was one chance remaining that you might both be drowned; and one chance that you might be recaptured before you could tell any one what you had seen. And there was a third chance that, if you should be recaptured, you might be persuaded to promise never to reveal what little of our secrets you already know. In that case, your lives might be spared, although not mine.

"So it was laid upon me to discover where you were, and to bring you back if possible. And on the polished table in that cave in which you saw Benares and Bombay and London and New York, I watched you swim down the river until you were rescued by the elephants.

"So then I went to meet you and bring you back."

"What if we had refused?"

"That elephant you rode — hah! One word from me, and the mob would have blamed you for the damage. They would have pulled you from the elephant and beaten you to death. Such processes are very simple to any one who understands mob-passions. Just a word — just a hint — and the rest is inevitable."

"But you say you are under sentence of death. What if you should refuse to obey them?"

"Why refuse? What good would that do?"

"But you were at liberty. Why not run away?"

"Whither? Besides, should I, who have enforced the penalty of death on so many fools, disloyal ones and fanatics, reject it for myself when I myself have failed? There is nothing unpleasant about death, my friend, although the manner of it may be terrible. But even torture is soon over; and the sting is gone from torture when the victim knows that the cause of science is thereby being advanced. They will learn from my agonies."

"Suit yourself!" I urged him. "Each to his own amusement. What happened after I turned to watch the elephant at the gate?"

"Those on whom the keeping of our secret rests considered that none would believe you, even if you were to tell what you have seen. But Athelstan King is different. For many years the Indian Government has accepted his bare word. Moreover, we knew that we can also accept his word. He is a man whose promises are as good as money, as the saying is.

"So after you turned aside to watch an elephant, those who were watching us opened a hidden door and Athelstan King was made prisoner from behind. They carried him bound and gagged into a cavern such as those you visited; and there he was confronted by the Nine Unknown, who asked him whether or not he will promise never to reveal what he had seen."

The Mahatma paused.

"Did he promise?" I asked him.

"He refused. What was more, he dared them to make away with him, saying that the mahout who had accompanied us hither would already have informed the Maharajah Jihanbihar, who would certainly report to the Government. And I, standing beside him, confirmed his statement."

"You seem to have acted as prosecuting attorney against yourself!" I said.

"No, I simply told the truth," he answered. "We who calculate in terms of eternity and infinity have scant use for untruth. I told the Nine Unknown the exact truth — that this man Athelstan King might not be killed, because of the consequences; and that whatever he might say to certain officers of the Government would be believed. So they let him go again, and set midnight tonight as the hour of the beginning of my death."

"Did King know that his refusal to promise entailed your death?" I asked.

He shook his head.

"Why didn't you tell him?"

"Because it would not have been true, my friend. I had already been sentenced to death. His promise could make no possible difference to my fate. They let him go, and ordered me to present myself at midnight; so I went with him, to preserve him from the cobras in a tunnel through which he must pass.

"I brought him into this palace by hidden ways, and after I had shown him the audience hall, where these princesses are to meet, he asked me to go and find you — that being easier for me than for him, because none in this palace would be likely to question me, whereas he would be detected instantly and watched, even if not prevented. And when I had found you — and you nearly killed me — some one, as you know, locked the door and shut us in here together. It is all one to me," he added with a shrug of the shoulders; "I have only until midnight at any event, and it makes small difference where I spend the intervening hours. Perhaps you would like to sleep a little? Why not? Sleep, and I will keep watch."

But, badly though I needed sleep, that sort of death-watch did not quite appeal. Besides, gentle, and honest and plausible though the Gray Mahatma now seemed, there was still something within me that rebelled at trusting him entirely. He had been all along too mysterious, and mystery is what irritates most of us more than anything else. It needs a man like Athelstan King to recognize the stark honesty of such a man as that Gray Mahatma; and Athelstan King was not there to set the example. I preferred to keep awake by continuing to question him.

"And d'you mean that those devils will deliberately torture you to death after you surrender voluntarily?" I asked.

"They are not devils," he answered solemnly.

"But they'll torture you?"

"What is called torture can hardly fail to accompany the process they will put me through — especially if I am to be honored as I hope. For a long time we have sought to make one experiment for which no suitable subject could be found. For centuries it has been believed that a certain scientific step is possible; but the subject on whom the experiment is tried must be one who knows all our secrets and well understands the manipulation of vibrations of the atmosphere. It is seldom that such an one has to be sentenced to death. And it is one of our laws that death shall never be imposed on any one not deserving of it. There are many, myself included, who would cheerfully have offered ourselves for that experiment at any time, had it been allowed."

"So you're really almost contented with the prospect?" I suggested.

"No, my friend. I am discontented. And for this reason. It may be that the nine unknown, who are obliged by the oath of our order to be stern and devoid of sentiment, will discover how pleased I would be to submit myself to that experiment. And in that case, in place of that experiment they would feel obliged merely to repeat some test that I have seen a dozen times."

"And throw your body to the alligators afterward?"

"In that case, yes. But if what I hope takes place, there will be nothing left for the alligators — nothing but bones without moisture in them that will seem ten centuries old."

CHAPTER XI

"KILL! KILL!"

The Gray Mahatma sat still, contemplating with apparent equanimity his end that should begin at midnight, and I sat contemplating him, when suddenly a new idea occurred to me.

"You intend to surrender to your executioners at midnight?" I asked him.

He nodded gravely.

"Suppose she keeps us locked in here; what then? You say you can't use your science to get out of here. What if you're late for the assignation?"

"You forget," he said with a deprecating gesture, "that they can see exactly where I am at any time! If they enter the cavern of vision and turn on the power they can see us now, instantly. They know perfectly well that my intention is to surrender to them. Therefore they will take care to make my escape from this place possible."

Five minutes later the door opened suddenly, and six women marched in. Two of them had wave-edged daggers, two had clubs, and the other two brought food and water. It was pretty good food, and there was enough of it for two; but the women would not say a word in answer to my questions.

They set the food and water down and filed out one by one, the last one guarding the retreat of all the rest and slipping out backward, pulling the door shut after her. Whereat I offered the Mahatma food and drink, but he refused the hot curry and only accepted a little water from the brass carafe.

"They will feed me special food tonight, for I shall need my strength," he explained; but the explanation was hardly satisfying.

I did not see how he could be any stronger later on for having let himself grow weaker in the interval. Nevertheless, I have often noticed this — that the East can train athletes by methods absolutely opposite to those imposed by trainers in the West, and it may be that their asceticism is based on something more than guesswork. I ate enormously, and he sat and watched me with an air of quiet amusement. He seemed to grow more and more friendly all the time, and to forget that he had made several attempts on my life, although his yellow eyes and lionlike way of carrying his head still gave you an uncomfortable feeling, not of mistrust but of incomprehension.

I began to realize how accurately King had summed him up; he was an absolutely honest man, which was why he was dangerous. His standards of conduct and motives were utterly different from ours, and he was honest enough to apply them without compromise or warning, that was all.

I was curious about his death sentence, and also anxious to keep awake, so I questioned him further, asking him point blank what kind of experiment they were going to try on him, and what would be the use of it. He meditated for about five minutes before answering:

"Is it within your knowledge that those who make guns seek ever to make them powerful enough to penetrate the thickest armor; and that the men who make armor seek always to make it strong enough to resist the most powerful guns, so that first the guns are stronger, and then the armor, and then the guns and then the armor again, until nations groan beneath the burden of extravagance? You know that?

"Understand, then, that that is but imitation of a higher law. A fragment of the force that we control is greater than the whole power of all the guns in the world, and forever we are seeking the knowledge of how to protect ourselves against it, so that we may safely experiment with higher potencies. As we learn the secret of safety we increase the power, and then learn more safety, and again increase the power. Perpetually there comes a stage at which we dare not go forward — yet — because we do not yet know what the result of higher potencies will be on our own bodies. Do you understand me? So. There will be an experiment tonight to ascertain the utmost limit of our present ability to resist the force."

"You mean they'll try the force on you?"

He nodded.

"Why not use an alligator? There are lots of creatures that die harder than a human being."

"It must be one who understands," he answered. "Not even a neophyte would do. It must be one of iron courage, who will resist to the last, enduring agony rather than letting in death that would instantly end the agony. It must be one who knows the full extent of all our knowledge, and can therefore apply all our present resources of resistance, so that the very outside edge of safety, as it were, may be measured accurately."

"And how long is the process likely to last?" I asked him.

"Who knows?" he answered. "Possibly three days, or longer. They will feed me scientifically, and will increase the potencies gradually, in order to observe the exact effects at different stages. And some of the more painful stages they will repeat again and again, because the greater the pain the greater the difficulty of registering exact degrees of resistance. The higher vibrations are not by any means always the most painful, any more than the brightest colors or the highest notes are always the most beautiful."

"Then you are to use your knowledge of resistance against their knowledge of force — is that it?"

He nodded.

"Isn't there a chance then that you may hold out to a point that will satisfy them? A point, I mean, at which you'll be more useful to them alive than dead? Surely if you should live and tell them all about it that would serve the purpose better than to have you dead and silent forever?"

He smiled like a school teacher turning down a promising pupil's suggestion.

"They will vibrate every atom of flesh and every drop of moisture from my bones before they have finished," he answered, "and they will do it as gradually as possible seeking to ascertain exactly the point at which human life ceases to persist. My part will be to retain my faculties to the very end, in order to exercise resistance to the last. So a great deal depends on my courage. It is possible that this experiment may carry science forward to a point where it commences a new era, for if we can learn to survive the higher potencies, a whole new realm will lie before us awaiting exploration."

"And if you refuse?"

"A dog's death!"

"Have they no use for mercy?"

"Surely. But mercy is not treason. It would be treason to the cause to let me live. I failed. I let the secret out. I *must* die. That is the law. If they let me live, the next one who failed would quote the precedent, and within a century or so a new law of compromise would have crept in. Our secrets would be all out, and the world would use our knowledge to destroy itself. No. They show their mercy by making use of me, instead of merely throwing my dead carcass to the alligators."

"If you will tell me your real name I will tell them at Johns

Hopkins about your death, and perhaps they will inscribe your record on some roll of martyrs," I suggested.

I think that idea tempted him, for his eyes brightened and grew strangely softer for a moment. He was about to speak, but at that moment the door opened again, and things began to occur that drove all thought of Johns Hopkins from our minds.

About a dozen women entered this time. They did not trouble to tie the Mahatma, but they bound me as the Philistines did Samson, and then threw a silken bag over my head by way of blindfold. The bag would have been perfectly effective if I had not caught it in my teeth as they drew it over my shoulders. It did not take long to bite a hole in it, nor much longer to move my head about until I had the hole in front of my right eye, after which I was able to see fairly well where they were leading me.

Women of most lands are less generous than men to any one in their power. Men would have been satisfied to let me follow them along or march in front of them, provided I went fast enough to suit them, but those vixens hardly treated me as human. Perhaps they thought that unless they beat, shoved, prodded and kicked me all the way along those corridors and up the gilded stairs I might forget who held the upper hand for the moment; but I think not. I think it was simply sex-venom — the half-involuntary vengeance that the under-dog inflicts on the other when positions are reversed. When India's women finally break purdah and enter politics openly, we shall see more cruelty and savagery, for that reason, than either the French or Russian terrors had to show.

I was bruised and actually bleeding in a dozen places when they hustled me down a corridor at last, and crowded me into a narrow anteroom, where the two harridans who had handled me hardest had the worst of it. I gave them what in elephant stables is known as the "squeeze," crushing them to right and left against projecting walls; whereat they screamed, and I heard the reproving voice of the Mahatma just behind me:

"Violence is the folly of beasts. Patience and strength are one!"

But they were not sticking pins into his ribs and thighs to humiliate and discourage him. He was being led by either hand, and cooed to softly in the sort of way that members of the Dorcas Guild would treat a bishop. It was easy enough for him to feel magnanimous. I managed to tread hard on one foot, and to squeeze two more women as they shoved me through a door into a vast audience hall, and the half-suppressed screams were music in my ears. I don't see why a woman who uses pins on a prisoner should be any more immune than a man from violent retaliation.

When they had shut the door they stripped the silk bag off over my head and holding me by the arms, four on either side, dragged me to the middle of a hall that was at least as large as Carnegie Hall in New York, and two or three thousand times as sumptuous.

I stood on a strip of carpet six feet wide, facing a throne that faced the door I had entered by. The throne was under a canopy, and formed the center of a horseshoe ring of gilded chairs, on every one of which sat a heavily veiled woman. Except that they were marvelously dressed in all the colors of the rainbow and so heavily jeweled that they flashed like the morning dew, there was nothing to identify any of the women except one. She was Yasmini. And she sat on the throne in the center, unveiled, unjeweled, and content to outshine all of them without any kind of artificial aid.

She sat under a hard white light directed from behind a lattice in the wall that would have exaggerated the slightest imperfection of looks or manner; and she looked like a fairy-book queen — like the queen you used to think of in the nursery when your aunt read stories to you and the illustrated Sunday supplements had not yet disillusioned you as to how queens wear their hats.

She was Titania, with a touch of Diana the Huntress, and decidedly something of Athena, goddess of wisdom, clothed in flowing cream that showed the outlines of her figure, and with sandals on her bare feet. Not a diamond. Not a jewel of any kind. Her hair was bound up in the Grecian fashion and shone like yellow gold.

Surely she seemed to have been born for the very purpose of presiding. Perhaps she was the only one who was at ease, for the others shifted restlessly behind their veils and had that vague, uncertain air that goes with inexperience — although one woman, larger looking than the rest, and veiled in embroidered black instead of colors, sat on a chair near the throne with a rather more nervy-looking outline. There were more than a hundred women in there all told.

Yasmini's change of countenance at sight of my predicament was instantaneous. I don't doubt it was her fault that I had been mistreated on the way up, for these women had seen me bound by her orders and mocked by her a couple of hours previously. But now she saw fit to seem indignant at the treatment I had suffered, and she made even the ranks of veiled princesses shudder as she rose and stormed at my captors, giving each word a sort of whip-lash weight.

"Shall a guest of mine suffer in my house?"

One of the women piped up with a complaint against me. I had trodden on her foot and crushed her against a door-jamb.

"Would he had slain you!" she retorted. "She-dog! Take her away! I will punish her afterward! Who stuck pins into him? Speak, or I will punish all of you!"

None owned up, but three or four of them who had not been able to come near enough to do me any damage betrayed the others, so she ordered all except four of them out of the room to await punishment at her convenience. And then she proceeded to apologize to me with such royal grace and apparent sincerity that I wondered whom she suspected of overhearing her. Wondering, my eyes wandering, I noticed the woman veiled in black. She was an elderly looking female, rather crouched up in her gorgeous shawl as if troubled with rheumatism, and neither her hands nor her feet were visible, both being hidden in the folds of the long *sari*.

The next instant Yasmini flew into a passion because the Mahatma and I were kept standing. The Mahatma was not standing, as a matter of fact; he had already squatted on the floor beside me. The women brought us stools, but the Mahatma refused his. Thinking I might be less conspicuous sitting than standing I sat down on my stool, whereat Yasmini began showering the women with abuse for not having supplied me with better garments. Considering the long swim, the dusty ride on an elephant, and two fights with women, during which they had been ripped nearly into rags, the clothes weren't half-bad!

So they brought me a silken robe that was woven all over with pictures of the Indian gods. And I sat feeling rather like a Roman, with that gorgeous toga wrapped around me; I might have been bearing Rome's ultimatum to the Amazons, supposing those belli-cose ladies to have existed in Rome's day.

But it was presently made exceedingly clear to me that Yasmini and not I was deliverer of ultimatums. She had the whole future of the world doped out, and her golden voice proceeded to herald a few of the details in mellifluous Punjabi.

"Princesses," she began, although doubtless some of them were not princesses, "this holy and benign Mahatma has been sentenced to die tonight, by those who resent his having trusted women with royal secrets. He is too proud to appeal for mercy; too indifferent to his own welfare to seek to avoid the unjust penalty. But there are others who are proud, and who are not indifferent!

"We women are too proud to let this Gray Mahatma die on our account! And it shall not be said of us that we consented to the death of the man who gave us our first glimpse of the ancient mysteries! I say the Gray Mahatma shall not die tonight!"

That challenge rang to the roof, and the women fluttered and thrilled to it. I confess that it thrilled me, for I did not care to think of the Mahatma's death, having come rather to like the man. The only person in the hall who showed no trace of the interest was the Mahatma himself, who squatted on the carpet close beside me as stolid and motionless as a bronze idol, with his yellow lion's eyes fixed on Yasmini straight ahead of him.

"These men, who think themselves omnipotent, who own the secret of the royal sciences," Yasmini went on, "are no less human than the rest of us. If I alone had learned the key to their secrets, they might have made an end of me, but there were others, and they did not know how many others! Now there are more; and not only women, but men! And not only men, but known men! Men who are known to the Government! Men whom they dare not try to make away with!

"It is true that if they should destroy the Gray Mahatma none would inquire for him, for he left the world behind him long ago, and none knows his real name or the place he can from. But that is not so in the case of these other men, one of whom sits beside him now. Already Maharajah Jihanbihar has inquired by telegraph as to their names and their business here, and the Government agents will be here within a day or two. Those two white men must be accounted for. Let them, then, account to us for the Gray Mahatma's life!"

I glanced sideways at the Gray Mahatma. He seemed perfectly indifferent. He was not even interested in the prospect of reprieve. I think his thoughts were miles away, although his eyes stared straight ahead at Yasmini. But he was interested in something, and I received the impression that he was waiting for that something to happen. His attitude was almost that of a telegraphist listening for sounds that have a meaning for him, but none for the common herd. And all at once I saw him nod, and beckon with a crooked forefinger.

There was nobody in that hall whom he was beckoning to. He was not nodding to Yasmini. I saw then that his eyes, although they looked straight at her, were focused beyond her for infinity. And there came to mind that chamber in the solid rock below the Tirthankers' temple in which the granite table stood on which whoever knew the secret could see anything, anywhere! I believe that I am as sane as you, who read this, and I swear that it seemed reasonable to me at that moment that the Gray Mahatma knew he was visible to watchers in that cavern, and that he was signaling to them to come and rescue him — from life, for the appointed death!

But Yasmini seemed not to have noticed any signaling, and if she did she certainly ignored it. Perhaps she believed that her hornet's nest of women could stand off any invasion or interference from without. At any rate, she went on unfolding her instructions to destiny with perfectly sublime assurance.

"It is only we women who can arouse India from the dream of the *Kali-Yug*. It is only in a free India that the Royal sciences can ever be stripped of their mystery. India is chained at present by opinions. Therefore opinions must be burst or melted! Melting is easier! It is hearts that melt opinions! Let these men, therefore, take this Gray Mahatma with them to the United States and let them melt opinions there! Let them answer to us for the Mahatma's life, and to us for the work they do yonder!

"And lest they feel that they have been imposed upon — that they are beggars sent to beg in behalf of beggars — let us pay them royally! Lo, there sits one of these men beside the Gray Mahatma. I invite you, royal women, to provide him with the wherewithal for that campaign to which we have appointed him and his friend!"

She herself set the example by throwing a purse at me — a leather wallet stuffed full of English banknotes, and the others had all evidently come prepared, for the room rained money for about two minutes! Purses fell on the Mahatma and on me in such profusion that surely Midas never felt more opulent — although the Mahatma took no notice of them even when one hit him in the face.

There were all kinds of purses, stuffed with all kinds of

money, but mostly paper money; some, however, had gold in them, for I heard the gold jingle, and the darned things hurt you when they landed like a rock on some part of your defenseless anatomy. Take them on the whole, those women made straight shooting, but not even curiosity was strong enough to make me pick up one purse and count its contents.

I rose and bowed acknowledgment without intending to commit myself, and without touching any of the purses, which would have been instantly interpreted as signifying acceptance. But I sat down again pretty promptly, for I had no sooner got to my feet than the woman in black got up too, and throwing aside the embroidered *sari* disclosed none other than Athelstan King looking sore-eyed from lack of sleep and rather weak from all he had gone through, but humorously determined, nevertheless.

Yasmini laughed aloud. Evidently she was in the secret. But nobody else had known, as the flutter of excitement proved. I think most of the women were rather deliciously scandalized, although some of them were so imbued with ancient prejudices that they drew their own veils all the closer and seemed to be trying to hide behind one another. In fact, any one interested in discovering which were the progressives and which the reactionaries in that assembly could have made a good guess in that minute, although it might not have done him much good unless he had a good memory for the colors and patterns of *saris*. A woman veiled in the Indian fashion is not easy to identify.

But before they could make up their minds whether to resent or applaud the trick that King had played on them with Yasmini's obvious collaboration, King was well under way with a speech that held them spellbound. It would have held any audience spellbound by its sheer, stark manliness. It was straighter from the shoulder than Yasmini's eloquence, and left absolutely nothing to imagination. Blunt, honest downrightness, that was the key of it, and it took away the breath of all those women used to the devious necessities of purdah politics.

"My friend and I refuse," he said, and paused to let them understand that thoroughly. "We refuse to accept your money."

Yasmini, who prided herself on her instantly ready wit, was too astonished to retort or to try to stop him. It was clear at a glance that she and King had had some sort of conference while the Mahatma and I were locked up together, and she had evidently expected King to fall in line and accept the trust imposed on him. Even now she seemed to think that he might be coming at concession in his own way, for her face had a look of expectancy. But King had nothing in his bag of surprises except disillusion.

"You see," he went on, "we can no longer be compelled. We might be killed, but that would bring prompt punishment. Maharajah Jihanbihar has already started inquiries about us, by telegraph, which, as you know, goes swiftly. We or else our slayers will have to be produced alive presently. So we refuse to accept orders or money from any one. But as for the Mahatma — we accord him our protection. There is only one power we recognize as able to impose death penalties. We repudiate all usurpation of that power. If the Mahatma thinks it will be safer in the United States, my friend and I will see that he gets there, at our expense.

"It was in my mind," he went on, "to drive a hard bargain with the Mahatma. I was going to offer him protection in return for knowledge. But it is not fair to drive bargains with a man so closely beset as he is. Therefore I offer him protection without terms."

With that he tossed the black *sari* aside and strode down the narrow carpet to where the Mahatma sat beside me, giving Yasmini a mere nod of courtesy as he turned his back on her. And until King reached us, the Mahatma squatted there beckoning one crooked forefinger, like a man trying to coax a snake out of its hole. King stood there smiling and looked down into his eyes, which suddenly lost their look of staring into infinity. He recognized King, and actually smiled.

"Well spoken!" he said rather patronizingly. "You are brave and honest. Your Government is helpless, but you and your friend shall live because of that offer you just made to me."

Yasmini was collecting eyes behind King's back, and it needed no expert to know that a hurricane was cooking; but King, who knew her temper well and must have been perfectly aware of danger, went on talking calmly to the Mahatma.

"You're reprieved too, my friend."

The Mahatma shook his head.

"Your Government is powerless. Listen!"

At that moment I thought he intended us to listen to Yasmini, who was giving orders to about a dozen women, who had entered the hall through a door behind the throne. But as I tried to catch the purport of her orders I heard another sound that, however distant, is as perfectly unmistakable as the boom of a bell, for instance, or any other that conveys its instant message to the mind. If you have ever heard the roar of a mob, never mind what mob, or where, or which language it roared in, you will never again mistake that sound for anything else.

"They have told the people," said the Mahatma. "Now the people will tear the palace down unless I am released. Thus I go free to my assignation."

We were not the only ones who recognized that tumult. Yasmini was almost the first to be aware of it; and a second after her ears had caught the sound, women came running in with word from Ismail that a mob was thundering at the gate demanding the Mahatma. A second after that the news had spread all through the hall, and although there was no panic there was perfectly unanimous decision what to do. The mob wanted the Mahatma. Let it have him! They clamored to have the Mahatma driven forth!

King turned and faced Yasmini again at last, and their eyes met down the length of that long carpet. He smiled, and she laughed back at him.

"Nevertheless," said the Mahatma, laying a hand on King's shoulder, and reaching for me with his other hand, "she is no more to be trusted than the lull of the typhoon. Come with me."

And with an arm about each of us he started to lead the way out through the maze of corridors and halls.

He was right. She was not to be trusted. She had laughed at King, but the laugh hid desperation, and before we reached the door of the audience hall at least a score of women pounced on King and me to drag us away from the Mahatma and make us prisoners again. And at that the Mahatma showed a new phase of his extraordinary character.

I was well weary by that time of being mauled by women. Suddenly the Mahatma seized my arm, and gave tongue in a resounding, strange, metallic voice such as I never heard before. It brought the whole surging assembly to rigid attention. It was a note of command, alarm, announcement, challenge, and it carried in its sharp reverberations something of the solemnity of an opening salvo of big guns. You could have heard a pin drop.

"I go. These two come with me. Shall I wait and let the mob come in to fetch me forth?"

But Yasmini had had time now in which to recover her self-possession, and she was in no mood to be out-generaled by any man whom she had once tricked so badly as to win his secrets from him. Her ringing laugh was an answering challenge, as she stood with one hand holding an arm of the throne in the attitude of royal arrogance.

"Good! Let the mob come! I, too, can manage mobs!"

Her voice was as arresting as his, although hers lacked the clamorous quality. There was no doubting her bravery, nor her conviction that she could deal with any horde that might come surging through the gates. But she was not the only woman in the room by more than ninety-nine and certainly ninety-nine of them were not her servants, but invited guests whom she had coaxed from their purdah strongholds partly by the lure of curiosity and partly by skilful playing on their new-born aspirations.

Doubtless her own women knew her resourcefulness and they might have lined up behind her to resist the mob. But not those others! They knew too well what the resulting reaction would be, if they should ever be defiled by such surging "untouchables" as clamored at the gate for a sight of their beloved Mahatma. To be as much as seen by those casteless folk within doors was such an outrage as never would be forgiven by husbands all too glad of an excuse for clamping tighter yet the bars of tyranny.

There was a perfect scream of fear and indignation. It was like the clamor of a thousand angry parrots, although there was worse in it than the hideous anger of any birds. Humanity afraid outscandals, outshames anything.

Yasmini, who would no more have feared the same number of men than if they had been trained animals, knew well enough that she had to deal now with something as ruthless as herself, with all her determination but without her understanding. It was an education to see her face change, as she stood and eyed those women, first accepting the challenge, because of her own indomitable spirit, then realizing that they could not be browbeaten into bravery, as men often can be, but that they must be yielded to if they were not to stampede from under her hand. She stood there reading them as a two-gun man might read the posse that had summoned him to surrender; and she deliberately chose surrender, with all the future chances that entailed, rather than the certain, absolute defeat that was the alternative. But she carried a high hand even while surrendering.

"You are afraid, all you women?" she exclaimed with one of her golden laughs. "Well — who shall blame you? This is too much to ask of you so soon. We will let the Mahatma go and take his friends with him. You may go!" she said, nodding regally to us three.

But that was not enough for some of them. The she-bear with her cubs in Springtime is a mild creature compared to a woman whose ancient prejudices have been interfered with, and a typhoon is more reasonable. Half-a-dozen of them screamed that two of us were white men who had trespassed within the purdah, and that we should be killed.

"Come!" urged the Mahatma, tugging at King and me. We went out of that hall at a dead run with screams of "Kill them! Kill them! Kill them!" shrilling behind us. And it may be that Yasmini conceded that point too, or perhaps she was unable to prevent, for we heard swift footsteps following, and I threw off that fifteen thousand dollar toga in order to be able to run more swiftly.

The Mahatma seemed to know that palace as a rat knows the runs among the tree-roots, and he took us down dark passages and stairs into the open with a speed that, if it did not baffle pursuit, at any rate made it easier for pursuers to pretend to lose us. Yasmini was no fool. She probably called the pursuit off.

We emerged into the same courtyard, where the marble stairs descended to the pool containing one great alligator. And we hurried from court to court to the same cage where the panther pressed himself against the bars, simultaneously showing fangs at King and me, and begging to have his ears rubbed. The Mahatma opened the cage-door, again using no key that I could detect, although it was a padlock that he unfastened and shoved the brute to one side, holding him by the scruff of the neck while King and I made swift tracks for the door at the back of the cage.

But this time we did not go through the tunnel full of rats and cobras. There was another passage on the same level with the courtyard that led from dark chamber to chamber until we emerged at last through an opening in the wall behind the huge image of a god into the gloom of the Tirthankers' temple — not that part of it that we had visited before, but another section fronting on the street.

And we could hear the crowd now very distinctly, egging one another on to commit the unforgivable offense and storm a woman's gates. They were shouting for the Gray Mahatma in chorus; it had grown into a chant already, and when a crowd once turns its collective yearnings into a single chant, it is only a matter of minutes before the gates go down, and blood flows, and all those outrages occur that none can account for afterward.

As long as men do their own thinking, decency and self-restraint are uppermost, but once let what the leaders call a slogan usher in the crowd-psychology, and let the slogan turn into a chant, and the Gardarene swine become patterns of conduct that the wisest crowd in the world could improve itself by imitating.

"Think! Think for yourselves!" said the Gray Mahatma, as if he recognized the thoughts that were occurring to King and me.

Then, making a sign to us to stay where we were, he left us and strode out on to the temple porch, looking down on the street that was choked to the bursting point with men who sweated and slobbered as they swayed in time to the chant of "Mahatma! O Mahatma! Come to us, Mahatma!"

King and I could see them through the jambs of the double-folding temple door.

The Mahatma stood looking down at them for about a minute before they recognized him. One by one, then by sixes, then by dozens they grew aware of him; and as that happened they grew silent, until the whole street was more still than a forest. They held their breath, and let it out in sibilant whispers like the voice of a little wind moving among leaves; and he did not speak until they were almost aburst with expectation.

"Go home!" he said then sternly. "Am I your property that ye break gates to get me? Go home!"

And they obeyed him, in sixes, in dozens, and at last in one great stream.

CHAPTER XII

THE CAVE OF BONES

The Gray Mahatma stood watching the crowd until the last sweating nondescript had obediently disappeared, and then returned into the temple to dismiss King and me.

"Come with us," King urged him; but he shook his head, looking more lionlike than ever, for in his yellow eyes now there was a blaze as of conquest.

He carried his head like a man who has looked fear in the face and laughed at it.

"I have my assignation to keep," he said quietly.

"You mean with death?" King asked him, and he nodded.

"Don't be too sure!"

King's retort was confident, and his smile was like the surgeon's who proposes to reassure his patient in advance of the operation. But the Mahatma's mind was set on the end appointed for him, and there was neither grief nor discontent in his voice as he answered.

"There is no such thing as being too sure."

"I shall use the telegraph, of course," King assured him. "If necessary to save your life I shall have you arrested."

The Mahatma smiled.

"Have you money?" he asked pleasantly.

"I shan't need money. I can send an official telegram."

"I meant for your own needs," said the Mahatma.

"I think I know where to borrow a few rupees," King answered. "They'll trust me for the railway tickets."

"Pardon me, my friend. It was my fault that your bag and clothes got separated from you. You had money in the bag. That shall be adjusted. Never mind how much money. Let us see how much is here."

That seemed a strange way of adjusting accounts, but there was logic in it nevertheless. There would be no use in offering us more than was available, and as for himself, he was naked except for the saffron smock. He had no purse, nor any way of hiding money on his person.

He opened his mouth wide and made a noise exactly like a bronze bell. Some sort of priest came running in answer to the summons and showed no surprise when given peremptory orders in a language of which I did not understand one word.

Within two minutes the priest was back again bearing a tray that was simply heaped with money, as if he had used the thing for a scoop to get the stuff out of a treasure chest. There was all kinds — gold, silver, paper, copper, nickel — as if those strange people simply threw into a chest all that they received exactly as they received it.

King took a hundred-rupee note from the tray, and the Gray Mahatma waved the rest aside. The priest departed, and a moment later I heard the clash and chink of money falling on money; by the sound it fell quite a distance, as if the treasure chest were an open cellar.

"Now," said the Gray Mahatma, placing a hand on the shoulders of each of us. "Go, and forget. It is not yet time to teach the world our sciences. India is not yet ripe for freedom. I urged them to move too soon. Go, ye two, and tell none what ye have seen, for men will only call you fools and liars. Above all, never seek to learn the secrets, for that means death — and there are such vastly easier deaths! Good-bye."

He turned and was gone in a moment, stepping sidewise into the shadows. We could not find him again, although we hunted until the temple priests came and made it obvious that they would prefer our room to our company. They did not exactly threaten us, but refused to answer questions, and pointed at the open door, as if they thought that was what we were looking for.

So we sought the sunlight, which was as refreshing after the temple gloom as a cold bath after heat, and turned first of all in the direction of Mulji Singh's apothecary, hoping to find that Yasmini had lied, or had been mistaken about that bag.

But Mulji Singh, although fabulously glad to see us, had no bag nor anything to say about its disappearance. He would not admit that we had left it there.

"You have been where men go mad, *sahibs*," was all the comment he would make.

"Don't you understand that we'll protect you against these people?" King insisted.

For answer to that Mulji Singh hunted about among the shelves for a minute, and presently set down a little white paper package on a corner of the table.

"Do you recognize that, *sahib*?" he asked.

"Deadly aconite," said King, reading the label.

"Can you protect me against it?"

"You're safe if you let it alone," King answered unguardedly.

"That is a very wise answer, *sahib*," said Mulji Singh, and set the aconite back on the highest shelf in the darkest corner out of reach.

So, as we could get nothing more out of Mulji Singh except a tonic that he said would preserve us both from fever, we sought the telegraph office, making as straight for it as the winding streets allowed. The door was shut. With my ear to a hole in the shutters I could hear loud snores within. King picked up a stone and started to thunder on the door with it.

The ensuing din brought heads to every upper window, and rows of other heads, like trophies of a ghastly hunt, began to decorate the edges of the roofs. Several people shouted to us, but King went on hammering, and at last a sleepy telegraph babu, half-in and half-out of his black alpaca jacket, opened to us.

"The wire is broken," he said, and slammed the door in our faces.

King picked up the stone and beat another tattoo.

"How long has the wire been broken?" he demanded.

"Since morning."

"Who sent the last message?"

"Maharajah Jihanbihar sahib."

"In full or in code?"

"In code."

He slammed the door again and bolted it, and whether or not he really fell asleep, within the minute he was giving us a perfect imitation of a hog snoring. What was more, the crowd began to take its cue from the babu, and a roof-tile broke at our feet as a gentle reminder that we had the town's permission to depart. Without caste-marks, and in those shabby, muddy, torn clothes, we were obviously undesirables.

So we made for the railroad station, where, since we had money, none could refuse to sell us third-class tickets. But, though we tried, we could not send a telegram from there either, although King took the station babu to one side and proved to him beyond argument that he knew the secret service signs. The babu was extremely sorry, but the wire was down. The trains were being run for the present on the old block system, one train waiting in a station until the next arrived, and so on.

So, although King sent a long telegram in code from a junction before we reached Lahore, nothing had been done about it by the time we had changed into Christian clothes at our hotel and called on the head of the Intelligence Department. And by then it was a day and a half since we had seen the Gray Mahatma.

The best part of another day was wasted in consulting and convincing men on whose knees the peace of India rested. They were naturally nervous about invading the sacred privacy of Hindu temples, and still more so of investigating Yasmini's doings in that nest of hers. There were men among them who took no stock in such tales as ours anyhow — hard and fast Scotch pragmatists, who doubted the sanity of any man who spoke seriously of anything that they themselves had not heard, seen, smelt, felt and tasted. Also there was one man who had been jealous of Athelstan King all his years in the service, and he jumped at the chance of obstructing him at last.

After we had told our story at least twenty times, more and more men being brought in to listen to it, who only served to increase incredulity and water down belief, King saw fit to fling his even temper to the winds and try what anger could accomplish. By that time there were eighteen of us, sitting around a mahogany table at midnight, and King brought his fist down with a crash that split the table and offended the dignity of than one man.

"Confound the lot of you!" he thundered. "I've been in the service twenty-one years and I've repeatedly brought back scores of wilder tales than this. But this is the first time that I've been disbelieved. I'm not in the service now. So here's my ultimatum! You take this matter up — at once — or I take it up on my own account! For one thing, I'll write a full account in all the papers of your refusal to investigate. Suit yourselves!"

They did not like it; but they liked his alternative less; and there were two or three men in the room, besides, who were secretly on King's side, but hardly cared to betray their opinions in the face of so much opposition. They did not care to seem too credulous. It was they who suggested with a half-humorous air of concession that no harm could be done by sending a committee of investigation to discover whether it were true that living men were held for experimental purposes beneath that Tirthanker temple; and one by one the rest yielded, somebody, however, imposing the ridiculous proviso that the Brahmin priests must be consulted first.

So, what with one thing and another, and one delay and another, and considering that the wire had been repaired and no less than thirty Brahmin priests were in the secret, the outcome was scarcely surprising.

Ten of us, including four policemen, called on the Maharajah Jihanbihar five full days after King and I had last seen the Mahatma; and after we had wasted half a morning in pleasantries and jokes about stealing a ride on his elephant, we rode in the Maharajah's two-horse landaus to the Tirthanker temple, where a priest, who looked blankly amazed, consented at once to be our guide through the sacred caverns.

But he said they were no longer sacred. He assured us they had not been used at all for centuries. And with a final word of caution against cobras he led the way, swinging a lantern with no more suggestion of anything unusual than if he had been our servant seeing us home on a dark night.

He even offered to take us through the cobra tunnel, but an acting deputy high commissioner turned on a flashlight and showed those goose-neck heads all bobbing in the dark, and that put an end to all talk of that venture, although the priest was cross-examined as to his willingness to go down there, and said he was certainly willing, and everybody voted that "deuced remarkable," but "didn't believe the beggar" nevertheless.

He showed us the "Pool of Terrors," filled with sacred alligators that he assured us were fed on goats provided by the superstitious townsfolk. He said that they were so tame that they would not attack a man, and offered to prove it by walking in. Since that entailed no risk to the committee they permitted him to do it, and he walked alone across the causeway that had given King and me such trouble a few nights before. Far from attacking him, the alligators turned their backs and swam away.

The committee waxed scornful and made numbers of jokes about King and me of a sort that a man doesn't listen to meekly is a rule. So I urged the committee to try the same trick, and they all refused. Then a rather bright notion occurred to me, and I stepped in myself, treading gingerly along the underwater causeway. And I was hardly in the water before the brutes all turned and came hurrying back — which took a little of the steam out of that committee of investigation. They became less free with their opinions.

So we all walked around the alligator pool by a passage that the priest showed us, and one by one we entered all the caves in which King and I had seen the fakirs and the victims undergoing torture.

The caves were the same, except that they were cleaner, and the ashes had all been washed away. There was nobody in them; not one soul, nor even a sign to betray that any one had been there for a thousand years.

There were the same cells surrounding the cavern in which the old fellow had sat reading from a roll of manuscript; but the cells were absolutely empty. I suggested taking flashlight photographs and fingerprint impressions of the doors and walls. But nobody had any magnesium, and the policemen said the doors might have been scrubbed in any case, so what was the use. And the priest with the lantern sneered, and the others laughed with him, so that King and I were made to look foolish once more.

Then we all went up to the temple courtyard, and descended the stairs through the hole in the floor of the cupola-covered stone platform. And there stood the lingam on its altar at the foot of the stairs, and there were the doors just as we had left them, looking as if they had been pressed into the molten stone by an enormous thumb. I thought we were going to be able to prove something of our story at last.

But not so. The priest opened the first door by kicking on it with his toe, and one by one we filed along the narrow passage in pitch darkness that was broken only by the swinging lantern carried by the man in front and the occasional flashes of an electric torch. King, one pace ahead of me, swore to himself savagely all the way, and although I did not feel as keenly as he did about it, because it meant a lot less to me what the committee might think, I surely did sympathize with him.

If we had come sooner it was beyond belief that we should not have caught those experts at their business, or at any rate in process of removing the tools of their strange trade. There must have been some mechanism connected with their golden light, for instance, but we could discover neither light nor any trace of the means of making it. Naturally the committee refused to believe that there had ever been any.

The caverns were there, just as we had seen them, only without their contents. The granite table, on which we had seen Benares, London and New York, was gone. The boxes and rolls of manuscript had vanished from the cavern in which the little ex-fat man had changed lead into gold before our eyes. The pit in the center of the cavern in which the fire-walkers had performed, still held ashes, but the ashes were cold and had either been slaked with water, or else water had been admitted into the pit from below. At any rate, the pit was flooded, and nobody wanted the job of wading into it to look for apparatus. So there may have been paraphernalia hidden under those ashes for aught that I know. It was a perfectly ridiculous investigation; its findings were not worth a moment's attention of any genuine scientist. Subsequently, newspaper editors wrote glibly of the gullibility of the human mind, with King's name and mine in full-sized letters in the middle of the article.

About the only circumstance that the investigating committee could not make jokes about was the cleanliness of all the passages and chambers. There was no dust, no dirt anywhere. You could have eaten off the floor, and there was no way of explaining how the dust of ages had not accumulated, unless those caverns had been occupied and thoroughly cleaned within a short space of time.

The air down there was getting foul already. There was no trace of the ventilation that had been so obvious when King and I were there before. Nevertheless, no trace could be found of any ventilating shaft; and that was another puzzle — how to account for the cleanliness and lack of air combined, added to the fact that such air as there was was still too fresh to be centuries old.

One fat fool on the committee wiped the sweat from the back of his neck in the lantern light and proposed at last that the committee should find that King and I had been the victims of delusion — perhaps of hypnotism. I asked him point blank what he knew about hypnotism. He tried to side-step the question, but I pinned him down to it, and he had to confess that he knew nothing about it whatever; whereat I asked each member of the committee whether or not he could diagnose hypnotism, and they all had to plead ignorance. So nobody seconded that motion.

King had lapsed into a sort of speechless rage. He had long been used to having his bare word accepted on any point whatever, having labored all his military years to just that end, craving that integrity of vision and perception that is so vastly more than honesty alone, that the blatant unbelief of these opinionative asses overwhelmed him for the moment.

There was not one man on the committee who had ever done anything more dangerous than shooting snipe, nor one who had seen anything more inexplicable than spots before his eyes after too much dinner. Yet they mocked King and me, in a sort of way that monkeys in the tree-tops mock a tiger.

Their remarks were on a par with those the cave-man must have used when some one came from over the sky-line and told them that fire could be made by rubbing bits of wood together. They recalled to us what the Gray Mahatma had said about Galileo trying to make the Pope believe that the earth moved around the sun. The Pope threatened to burn Galileo for heresy; they only offered to pillory us with public ridicule; so the world has gone forward a little bit.

"Let's go," said somebody at last. "I've had enough of this. We're trespassing, as well as heaping indignity on estimable Hindus."

"Go!" retorted King. "I wish you would! Leave Ramsden and me alone in here. There's a cavern we haven't seen yet. You've formed your opinions. Go and publish them; they'll interest your friends."

He produced a flashlight of his own and led the way along the passage, I following. The committee hesitated, and then one by one came after us, more anxious, I think, to complete the fiasco than to unearth facts.

But the door that King tried to open would not yield. It was the only door in all those caverns that had refused to swing open at the first touch, and this one was fastened so rigidly that it might have been one with the frame for all the movement our blows on it produced. Our guide swore he did not know the secret of it, and our letter of authority included no permission to break down doors or destroy property in any way at all.

It looked as though we were blocked, and the committee were all for the air and leaving that door unopened. King urged them to go and leave it — told them flatly that neither they nor the world would be any wiser for anything whatever that they might do — was as beastly rude, in fact, as he knew how to be; with the result that they set their minds on seeing it through, for fear lest we should find something after all that would serve for an argument against their criticism.

Neither King nor I were worried by the letter of the committee's orders, and I went to look for a rock to break the door down with. They objected, of course, and so did the priest, but I told them they might blame the violence on me, and furthermore suggested that if they supposed they were able to prevent me they might try. Whereat the priest did discover a way of opening the door, and that was the only action in the least resembling the occult that any of us saw that day.

There were so many shadows, and they so deep, that a knob or trigger of some kind might easily have been hidden in the darkness beyond our view; but the strange part was that there was no bolt to the door, nor any slot into which a bolt could slide. I believe the door was held shut by the pressure of the surrounding rock, and that the priest knew some way of releasing it.

We entered a bare cavern which was apparently an exact cube of about forty feet. It was the only cavern in all that system of caverns whose walls, corners, roof and floor were all exactly smooth. It contained no furniture of any kind.

But exactly in the middle of the floor, with hands and feet pointing to the four corners of the cavern, was a grown man's skeleton, complete to the last tooth. King had brought a compass with him, and if that was reasonably accurate then the arms and legs of the skeleton were exactly oriented, north, south, east and west; there was an apparent inaccuracy of a little less than five degrees, which was no doubt attributable to the pocket instrument.

One of the committee members tried to pick a bone up, and it fell to pieces in his fingers. Another man touched a rib, and that broke brittlely. I picked up the broken piece of rib and held it in the rays of King's flashlight.

"You remember?" said King in an undertone to me. "You recall the Gray Mahatma's words? 'There will be nothing left for the alligators!' There's neither fat nor moisture in that bone, it's like chalk. See?"

He squeezed it in his fingers and it crumbled.

"Huh! This fellow has been dead for centuries," said somebody. "He can't have been a Hindu, or they'd have burned him. No use wondering who *he* was; there's nothing to identify him with — no hair, no clothing — nothing but dead bone."

"Nothing! Nothing whatever!" said the priest with a dry laugh, and began kicking the bones here and there all over the cavern. They crumbled as his foot struck them, and turned to dust as he trod on them — all except the teeth. As he kicked the skull across the floor the teeth scattered, but King and I picked up a few of them, and I have mine yet — two molars and two incisors belonging to a man, who to my mind was as much an honest martyr as any in Fox's book.

"Well, Mr. King," asked one of the committee in his choicest note of sarcasm, "have you any more marvels to exhibit, or shall we adjourn?"

"Adjourn by all means," King advised him.

"We know it all, eh?"

"Truly, you know it all," King answered without a smile.

Then speaking sidewise in an undertone to me:

"And you and I know nothing. That's a better place to start from, Ramsden. I don't know how you feel, but I'm going to track their science down until I'm dead or master of it. The very highest knowledge we've attained is ignorance compared to what these fellows showed us. I'm going to discover their secret or break my neck!"

THE END

www.ingramcontent.com/pod-product-compliance
Lightning Source LLC
Chambersburg PA
CBHW020659180626
46816CB00003B/1359